Penguin Science Fiction
The Last Refuge

John Petty was born in Shropshire in 1919. He left school when he was fourteen for economic reasons and slaved for a pittance in a barber's shop. After this he worked for two years in foundries and factories, then joined the army, where conditions were so bad that he deserted and made his way to London. 'I had a variety of experience being a down-and-out', then he worked in a hospital. When the war came he was recalled and (after eighty-four days' detention) served in the army before being invalided out. He was assistant foreman in a Bombay foundry when a disastrous breakdown in health changed his life both physically and psychologically. He began to write his autobiography, *Five Fags a Day*, and until it was published in 1957 he was a scrap-picker. *Five Fags a Day* was acclaimed by the critics, and was followed by a novel, *A Flame in My Heart*. He has also contributed to the *Birmingham Post*, the *Guardian*, and many other newspapers and journals.

John Petty is tall, dark and lean. He likes to go for country walks, and enjoys listening to the rubbish men talk in pubs.

John Petty

The Last Refuge

Penguin Books

All of the characters in this
book are fictitious and any resemblance to
actual persons, living or dead, is
purely coincidental

Penguin Books Ltd, Harmondsworth,
Middlesex, England
Penguin Books Australia Ltd, Ringwood,
Victoria, Australia

First published by Ronald Whiting & Wheaton 1966
Published in Penguin Books 1968

Made and printed in Great Britain by
C. Nicholls & Company Ltd
Set in Intertype Times

Cover design by Richard Hollis, using a photograph from
Geology (Oxford University Press)

To my wife
Snowy and Mick

Chapter 1

The Housing Department inquiry office was deceptively homely, a small cosy room with a glowing stove and an elderly, kindly looking man behind the counter. But the room into which Muller was shown was different, a cold room furnished only with a desk and two chairs. There wasn't even a filing cabinet. The Estate Superintendent went out and returned within seconds with a large folio. He placed it on the desk and Muller licked his lips.

The Estate Superintendent was tall, six feet two or three with a bulbous nose and grey eyes. They were cold eyes, smallish, and suited the Superintendent's lean, forbidding face. But for the nose he would have been quite fierce, something like a picture of an old Arab chief Muller had seen years ago.

The Superintendent glanced through the dossier, sighing sombrely now and then. Although it was so clammily cold Muller started to sweat.

'Well, Mr Muller,' the Superintendent said at last. 'You know the position.'

'Er, yes,' said Muller, nerves making his voice shrill. He didn't know the position, but so far as he knew none of the others had been sent for.

'Thirty years ago,' said the Superintendent, 'there were 27,982 houses in this town, 12,742 municipal dwellings and the rest privately owned. Today there are –' his voice rose – 'only 223 houses left. There's progress for you.'

Muller nodded. His mouth was dry. The Superintendent contemplated the ceiling. He didn't speak for fully a minute. 'Don't believe much in progress, do you?'

Muller gulped. 'Progress. Oh yes. I hadn't – I mean –

I've *always* believed in progress, true progress, but the amount of money that was squandered – not squandered, er, er, *spent* on things of doubtful value, spent er –'

'*Doubtful?*' interjected the Superintendent.

Muller tried to pause, tried to take a breath. He was afraid, and it hadn't helped him years ago when he had lost his temper with the wrong people at the wrong time.

'Doubtful to me,' he managed. 'It was just my opinion. And –' he tried to laugh – 'my opinion didn't matter much.'

'Not *much*,' said the Superintendent softly – a shade too softly.

'But that was years ago,' croaked Muller. 'I was young and – well, I was, I was *young* and it *was* a long time ago.'

He eased his collar, which was by no means tight; and the Superintendent laughed, a laugh that became a jeer.

'Mr Muller,' he said, 'I've been looking at some of your old writings. You were a pretty violent reactionary. As a matter of fact,' said the Superintendent – quite expansively, 'when I sat for my diploma I had to write a paper on Social Movements in this century and that meant a lot of study. And,' said the Superintendent, 'I tried a lot of old books and articles and whatnot written from 1900 onwards – in the nineteen-tens and nineteen-twenties and nineteen-thirties. AND,' said the Superintendent, 'I read nothing as reactionary as yours.' He stood up. 'But,' he said coldly, 'all those men and women were disturbed by poverty. It was mainly that: poverty. And things like that had been resolved by the time you were writing, but you were violently reactionary. Why?'

Muller's face was burning, but he knew it was probably the colour of clay.

'A rebel,' said the Superintendent, 'not only without a cause but a rebel trying to create a cause, and a wrong one at that.'

You're going out, Muller told himself. For a long time you've been going out, and the end isn't far off.

'There was a cause,' he said.

The Superintendent's brows lifted. 'My own unhappiness,' said Muller.

The Superintendent stared for a long time. '*Unhappiness?*'

'It makes for causes. And,' said Muller, 'because I was so unhappy and – well, never very well-off – I saw people instead of buildings and I knew the Great Change hadn't changed life for the better. For the young, perhaps, yes, but many older people had a thin time paying for the Change. They weren't prosperous and they weren't happy.'

That was more like his old self. His heart was hammering and he was visibly shaking but he felt better. The Superintendent fell into a trance-like contemplation.

'I'm being honest,' said Muller.

The Superintendent stirred and sighed. Very gently he sighed. '*Mister* Muller,' he said, almost with pity, 'we didn't *ask* for the nuclear war of the nineteen-seventies. We didn't ask for it, but we did have to rehouse twenty million people. That called for something of an effort, didn't it?'

'For rebuilding, yes,' said Muller. He was horribly nervous again. 'For a change. But we tried to change life instead of destroying the armaments industry.'

The Superintendent sighed again. 'I thought sentimentalists like you were a thing of the past.' And he flipped through the dossier and said briskly: 'But all this is irrelevant. As I was saying, there are 223 houses left in this town and they've got to come down. It was the intention to preserve them as curios, museum pieces, but there it is: the Committee want the ground.'

'What – for?' asked Muller.

'That's none of your business,' said the Superintendent gloomily.

'But ...' said Muller, 'there's so much land vacant. I mean ...'

'Mean what?'

'There are only about 70,000 people and they're housed very compactly. The town occupies less than a third of –'

'You're at your old game, aren't you?' the Superintendent interrupted. 'Challenging authority and questioning decisions.'

'I was just wondering,' said Muller.

The Superintendent stared. 'Some members of the Committee,' he said slowly, 'wanted to classify you as an enemy of society, but the general feeling was that you weren't important enough – and never had been – to be so classified. But,' said the Superintendent, 'you're dangerously near to being classified as totally undesirable, and you know what that means.'

Muller knew; the end was the same.

*

He was so rigid that a pebble flung against him would have shattered him. Smashed him to fragments. Or that was how he felt.

'Personally,' the Superintendent said softly, 'I see all sides of the question. I have to, in my job. And I see you' – he waved – 'as a man who would have been complete and happy if you had lived a century ago. One of those old Socialists agitating against what they thought was injustice. But,' said the Superintendent, 'you can't live in the past and you can't live in the future. You have to live in the present and accept life as it is. And,' said the Superintendent with finality, 'a child of six doesn't have to be told that, but there's a copy of a medical report in your dossier pointing out that very thing, and that was seventeen years ago.' Muller tried to speak. It took an effort. 'I – I've never lived in the past. It's just that – that you see things differently and people say "You should have lived centuries ago", and others say "Oh, you are in advance of your time".'

He gulped.

'But – that's how it was years ago. In my youth, I mean. Why,' said Muller, 'I can remember the time when I had twenty or thirty letters a day. It took an effort to keep up with them. But now' – their eyes met – 'people write very rarely. Instead of twenty or thirty letters a day there might be two in a week, often not that. I,' said Muller, 'don't matter now.'

'No,' agreed the Superintendent.

'I never did matter to most people.' It hurt, even now, to say that. 'But I don't matter at all now. Why bother about me? Why not leave me in peace?'

The Superintendent's face lifted affirmatively, but he spoke sternly. 'You're being childish, Muller. You know as well as I do that it's this question of re-accommodation. There are two hundred and twenty-three houses in this town and they're coming down. Two hundred and twenty-two are occupied by orthodox families of the artisan type and their re-accommodation gives no problem at all. They'll be diverted to Blocks R and S and that will be that. No problems at all.'

Muller winced.

'I suppose,' the Superintendent said sarcastically, 'that you'd like to be directed to Blocks A or B, but we hardly think you suitable.'

Blocks A and B were purely residential, occupied mainly by professional people.

'You haven't the income,' the Superintendent said bleakly. 'You haven't the history and you haven't the background.'

'Background?' Muller queried.

For answer the Superintendent touched a button beneath the desk and a dry, weak voice crept into the room.

'On April 29th 1998 I inspected number seven Queen Street. This house is occupied by James Muller. Externally the front of the house was drab; the – er – garden [gardens, of course, generally speaking, were a thing of the past] seemed in good order, but the curtains were shabby and tattered and the door knocker was missing. Parts of the fence were missing. Although unimpressed I wasn't prejudiced because as I say some effort had been made to maintain the frontal appearance. The garden had been worked over recently. But the house at the rear shocked me. One downstairs window and four upstairs windows were broken. The garden was a mess. Bottles and other rubbish lay about. Beneath some sort of bush were tea-leaves. The tenant must empty his tea-pot there. The fence in places was broken and the drain –'

The Superintendent switched the voice off and said woodenly, 'A written copy of that report has been seen by the Committee.'

Muller's head was pounding.

'But good God!' he choked. 'This is mad! Crazy! I removed the door knocker because the kids keep on thumping it. There's a rough family next door with a horde of kids and they've made my life a misery. Thump the knocker and run away. Throw stones at the windows and break them.'

'*Stones?*' queried the Superintendent.

'Pebbles. Bricks. Things out of the soil. The ground. They throw their rubbish over and make bonfires from the fencing, which is about fifty years old and rot –' Muller paused and said desperately: 'Bonfires! You've heard of bonfires! There used to be a thing known as bonfire night. Fifth of November!'

The Superintendent stared.

'So much for the fencing. I do my best but it's impossible keeping up with those kids. I clean the drain every morning but the wind blows the rubbish about. Paper and whatnot. And as for the garden I used to have a lovely garden – I happen to like gardens – but –'

The Superintendent smirked.

'All right,' said Muller. 'I know! I know! Gardens and flowers and so on are old-fashioned. A thing of the past. Everything is produced synthetically now and animal and vegetable life is a thing of the past. You concreted the countryside over to keep it tidy and –'

'For military and scientific reasons,' the Superintendent said sternly.

'All right. Using synthetic concrete. But in effect you're

criticizing me for being old-fashioned and that's just what my house is. It's seventy years old. So are the others for that matter. They're about seventy years old. And everything of which you complain couldn't happen in the new blocks – it just couldn't happen. The new blocks haven't door knockers or gardens or fences or drains and they certainly haven't uncontrolled young hooligans. The rubbish – the salvage – is disposed of sci—'

The Superintendent laughed. He laughed loudly but he wasn't amused.

'Muller,' he said. 'You like old-fashioned things but you won't keep them in good order. See?'

'But I do,' Muller said desperately. 'I do! You just wouldn't believe what efforts I've made. But that family next –'

'It's no use blaming anything on the people next door. You're the tenant. You're responsible.'

'But – but – don't you see how *absurd* it is? The drain's an open drain, you know, and paper and leaves and so on blow into it, but I clean it out every morning. And I throw the tea-leaves outside because it seems the cleanest thing to do.'

'*Cleanest?*' said the Superintendent, quite startled.

'Certainly. To me anyway. The sink's not much good – the pipe's too narrow and gets blocked very easily. There's the waste bin outside, of course, but emptying a tea-pot into it first thing in the morning. Well,' said Muller, 'I'm afraid I'm touchy-stomached.'

'I'm not,' said the Superintendent.

'But that's the point,' urged Muller. 'I loathe sordidness, and tea-leaves scattered about *is* a disgusting sight. But every few days I get the spade and dig them into the garden. It only takes two or three minutes.'

'I see,' said the Superintendent. 'But it would take more than a few minutes to replace the broken windows.'

'But I *have* replaced windows,' Muller said despairingly. 'A dozen times and more I've replaced windows. But those kids break windows faster than I can replace them – and faster than I can afford to replace them.'

'I know that,' the Superintendent said softly.

'But I *try*,' said Muller. 'I *try*. It's been hell since the Sullivans came to live next door. But I do try to repair their vandalism. Fences are a thing of the past and fencing materials are almost impossible to obtain, but I've done my best to plug gaps in that fence. I've used sticks from trees and so on.'

'Sticks?'

'Boughs. Branches. And –' he was sweating but he did feel more confident – 'logic and advocacy were never my strong points, but the Fanshawes live on one side of me and the Sullivans on the other. I live in a terrace; they used to be called terraced houses. And,' said Muller, 'the fence on the Fanshawes' side is in excellent condition because the Fanshawes are people like that. But the fence on the Sullivan's side is a mess because the Sullivans are vandals. Yet it's their fence as much as mine. It's a common fence; it partitions one garden from the other. But I get the blame.'

The Superintendent stared steadily before him.

'As a matter of fact,' said Muller, 'talking about drains and rubbish and whatnot, the Sullivans' house isn't just a mess; it stinks. The house, not just the garden. It stinks, it reeks; but the Sullivans don't seem to have been carpeted.'

The Superintendent sighed. Very gently he sighed. 'It's a good thing these old houses are coming down. They are a thing of the past, and some of you who live in them have preserved the faults of a bygone age.'

'That's possible,' said Muller, 'but it's no answer.'

The Superintendent stood up.

'Mr Sullivan's a good workman. There's never been a bad mark against him. And he's the father of eight children. The State wants children, Muller. You're not even married.'

*

He walked round the desk and stood menacingly. 'Any faults the Sullivans may have will be quickly remedied in Block S. Very quickly and very thoroughly remedied.'

He was suddenly frightening but he sat down again quietly.

He opened the dossier at the first page. 'This house of yours. The tenancy passed to you when your parents died?'

Muller couldn't speak.

'Five years ago. I was away at the time. Remedial measures should have been taken then.'

Muller didn't speak.

'Your father –' the Superintendent struggled with unfamiliar words, and Muller said he was German.

'What?'

'German.'

For a second the Superintendent stared blankly (Germany, with Russia and the United States, had been totally destroyed in the nuclear war) and Muller said his father was born in Germany.

'Germany?'

'Yes. He was a sailor.'

'And your mother was a local woman.'

'They met,' Muller said sombrely – he still missed his parents very much – 'in London. It was my mother's first visit to London. And the last of course. My father was on leave. His ship was down river.'

The Superintendent seemed doubtful.

'He was,' Muller said, 'a merchant seaman. He was a man of peace. What happened later wasn't his fault. He didn't drop the bombs. He didn't even make them.'

'Maybe,' said the Superintendent. 'But it doesn't help. Nothing in your case helps.'

'Even if it doesn't, don't blame it on my father. Or my mother, who wasn't too young when I was born, and very far from well. My faults, if faults they are,' Muller snapped, 'stem exclusively from the English side.'

He was trembling with anger and the Superintendent looked at him clinically.

'You know, Muller,' he murmured, 'you may not accept this but you just about owe your life to me. I do carry some weight with the Committee and there's no doubt you would have been put down if I had gone sharply against you. But you interest me.'

Muller licked his lips.

'You have never,' the Superintendent continued, 'had much of a foundation. Your education was ordinary. You have never had much money. You have no wife or children and according to the dossier you haven't one living relative. They're all dead. In addition you've had quite a lot of ill-health and to *look* at' – the Superintendent's voice rose – 'to look at you're a miserable little devil.'

There was a silence.

'I don't mean,' the Superintendent qualified, 'that you look *miserable*. For your age and history you're surprisingly young-looking. But you're thin and smallish and stoop-shouldered – there isn't a modern boy of thirteen who isn't better developed. You're a poor physical specimen and you don't look well. But you've always been noted for the violence and vigour of your opinions.'

Muller had to do something. He stood up. 'It's not that I'm brave or a natural revolutionary. I – I was never meant for the practical side of things at all. It's – it's just the way I am. When things have seemed wrong I've said so.'

'And they're wrong now?'

'Wrong?' said Muller, and sat down. 'Wrong? I'm small, you say?'

'Smallish – physically.'

'I'm five feet nine with my stoop – which is slight and caused by bending over too many books. Five-nine wouldn't have been thought a bad height years ago.'

'It's not important. I've seen smaller men.'

'But I'm smallish you say and –' Muller paused . . . 'I *do* like small things. Years ago there were large things. Art and landscapes and great oceans. Immensity in nature is awesome and so is great art. But –' it was time for Muller's own voice to rise – 'landscapes are no more and oceans for the most part are hidden. And our houses are to come down and I don't care for vast erections. I like my buildings small.'

'Small?' said the Superintendent woodenly.

'I feel better,' said Muller, 'or, rather, *felt* better. It's probably just a question of neurosis, but when there was a choice I felt better in small shops than large shops, and small pubs than large pubs. It's not,' said Muller, 'that I liked smallness in itself, and God knows I don't like smallness in men or values. I just felt better. Less neurotic, more at ease somehow.'

The Superintendent shook his head.

'It's simple, my lad. The large buildings triggered off some fear in you. Insecurity, I suppose. And it could have been put right very easily.'

'Perhaps. But' – Muller stared at the big man's nose – 'there was something about those small pubs. Do you remember the atmosphere?'

'No, I don't,' the Superintendent snapped irritably. 'And I find our Halls of Pleasure adequate in every way.'

'They're made to hold three thousand people.'

'What of it? In the old days ocean liners carried three or four thousand people. All jammed together in one vessel.'

'But not in one room.'

For a moment the Superintendent seemed angry, then he laughed.

'It's funny, Muller. You have held outrageous ideas and you must have had courage. But you're the nervous type and feel better in little old buildings.'

He jumped up and pondered briefly, then shook his head.

'They wouldn't have it. The Committee haven't any understanding of people like you. Personally,' he said, sighing heavily, 'I think you're harmless and I'd be prepared to transfer you to Block B or C, and supplement your income adequately. On condition, of course, that you lived quietly and kept your crackpot ideas to yourself. But –' he spread his hands and sat down.

Muller waited.

'You wrote some original books. They were good, but

your ideas were revolutionary politically, not artistically. And to be a successful rebel you must appeal to a majority of people or to a large section of people. You didn't. Your theories were reactionary, not progressive.'

'Progressive?' Muller mumbled.

'People,' the Superintendent said smoothly, 'have always gone for the big, shiny *new* things. That's progress, Muller, or a part of it.'

'And science has never been more advanced. And politics are a thing of the past. And,' said Muller, reddening again, 'we live in a time of terror. People have never been more afraid.'

'Only of oblivion.'

'Only!'

'Science is advanced, as you say, and it's not our fault if it has got into the hands of the wrong people. People,' said the Superintendent, 'as irresponsible as your neighbour's children.'

'They are children!' Muller exploded. 'The great nations have gone but now a few science students mucking about in Accra or Bangkok can –'

The Superintendent stopped him.

'Yes. But with such a situation –'

'Brought about by progress!'

'By the mistakes of years ago,' the Superintendent retorted. 'We can't go back, Muller. You'd like to live in the eighteenth century and even *that* has been advocated.'

'*Advocated?*'

'Certainly. To destroy modern civilization and to start again with wagons and horses. Love that, wouldn't you, Muller? Lanterns and candlelight. But,' said the Superintendent, 'there are no horses left, and if we could revert to a rustic age someone would rig up a laboratory and off we'd go again. So we must progress. And achieve perfection or perish.'

'No halfway house?'

'None. Searching all the time of course for the perfect

weapon. Something that can't be intercepted or nullified and something that will destroy totally.'

'Cosy prospect, isn't it?' said Muller. 'Scientists all over the world – or what's left of it – searching for the perfect weapon.'

'It's a race of course. And I think we'll win. *After* we've won we may even get back to the humanities and to eccentrics such as you. In the meantime the situation is tricky and,' the Superintendent said gravely, 'people are bound to be edgy, the police particularly.'

Muller's heart sank. Now and then during the conversation he had been hopeful, but he knew he had been deluding himself; the police couldn't be excluded.

'After all,' the Superintendent continued, 'we must be fair. The police have always had to be more careful and suspicious than most people – inevitably. It was inevitable in the days when their main function was dealing with crime, and now that they're responsible for security . . . well . . . what Mr Jallen would make of you I don't know.'

*

Jallen was the Chief of Police. He was tall, very thin, with a scarred, pallid face unusually long and thin. Muller had seen his picture often, it wasn't easy to escape it, and a year or so back he had seen the man. It was a lovely evening in May, and Muller had decided to go for a walk, not a thing he did often nowadays. He had never been one to walk aimlessly, even when there had been fields and flowers to look at, and the authorities certainly didn't approve of people walking about aimlessly.

I might as well go back, Muller had told himself before he reached the corner, when he had bumped into Mr and Mrs Andrews, a jolly old couple – few like them left – and they insisted he spend the evening with them. Muller had at first declined, but he hadn't wished to offend Mrs Andrews. He liked her, and she was helpful, doing his shopping for him. 'Not that *your* groceries are much of a burden,' she used to laugh, but the point was, of course, that all shopping and other facilities were now concentrated within the new blocks, and because of this the residents of the old houses had passes admitting them to Block R.

'Now come on, you old hermit,' she laughed. 'You never go out at all and a bit of a change will do you good.'

'I'd really rather not,' Muller said, but Mr Andrews took his arm earnestly.

'You ought to, you know. Have you thought how lucky we are to have our own little houses?'

'I have indeed.'

'But for how long? They're bound to come down sooner or later. And I'll bet you haven't been inside Block R three times. You might just as well get used to the new blocks now. You'll *have* to live in one sooner or later.'

'Let's hope it's later,' Mrs Andrews said comfortingly. 'And now let's go and have a drink.'

The Hall of Pleasure was packed. The heat and noise was terrific. And the Andrews – healthy extroverts who loved a crowd – walked past Bar 1 and Bar 2 and Bar 3 and Bar 4 until they were in the thick of a perspiring mass of humans. The walk across the vast room had made Muller light-headed, and two quick drinks gave him no relief. He started to sweat and the swirling smoke choked him. McAllister had told him the ventilation and air-conditioning plants in the Halls of Pleasure of all blocks below C were switched off (and the temperature raised) for an hour now and then, and Muller hadn't believed him. 'But it does them good,' McAllister had said. 'They work up the most hell of a sweat, particularly as the booze is loaded. Does them a world of good.' Muller was sceptical: it was so crude. Even nowadays, he said, people wouldn't drink if the stuff was drugged. McAllister had laughed. 'You're so damn naïve. Maybe it's because you live in that damn little house, breathing God's unadulterated air. You won't be so damn pure after you've had a few weeks of inhaling the controlled stuff they pump into the new blocks.' Muller was sceptical. 'It is so crude. Isn't this supposed to be the age of scientific perfection? And aren't people supposed to be healthier than ever before?' McAllister had sighed. 'They don't do it *all* the time. Maybe once or twice a week. The chief copper uses his discretion. When people look extra tired and nervy he gives the order. An hour or so later they're all like dish cloths in a turkish bath and cockeyed happy into the bargain. Bang go their fears and inhibitions. Isn't that doing them good?'

They certainly seemed to like it. Laughing and shouting, they all gave an impression of crude and uncomplicated content. There wasn't one unhappy face and there wasn't one unhealthy face. Neither was there one attractive face. The Andrews, such nice old people, were bawling away like drunks at a boxing-match, the sweat streaming down their faces that were already a dark rose red. Muller saw that McAllister was right. In an age of almost total control and repression an occasional work-out was beneficial. 'Trouble is that you're clever,' McAllister had said, 'and you expect most everyone else to be clever, particularly as this is an age of scientific marvels. But most people aren't as clever or even cleverer than they used to be; they're a damn sight stupider, and that's how they have to be handled. Simply but firmly.'

McAllister, as a teacher (somewhat unorthodox; he had been transferred abruptly), should know, but Muller didn't like it and he couldn't stand it. He could taste the sweat at the corners of his mouth and the noise was so overpowering that he could feel it, literally. His eardrums throbbed, and when he groped towards Mrs Andrews, sound waves vibrated, or seemed to vibrate, on his fingers.

'I must go,' he shouted, but she didn't hear him. 'I'm sorry I must go,' he shouted and strode away. He was so light-headed he almost fainted. It was like fighting through a scrimmage getting to the doors and he sank down heavily in Bar 1 Annexe. For a while he just sat, then he inserted a coin and dialled and drank deeply when the pint of bitter appeared. It was almost as hot here, but less smoky and much quieter. Few people were in the Annexe and Muller began to feel better. 'After all,' he thought, 'the authorities don't compel people to sit in the main Hall, they go in there of their own free will.' He drained his glass and inserted another coin in the slot below the table; it was fascinating to see the refill rise towards him. He looked around him. There were a few men, elderly most of them, and opposite him, one couple. They took Muller's eye at once because the man was obviously middle-class and the woman was a poor old thing very much older. The man was hatless, casually but comfortably dressed, and his face made Muller blink. It was pale, naturally distinctive and obviously authoritative, and Muller hesitated because he had always seen the face pictured with a black peaked cap low over the eyes. Yes, of course, it was Jallen, the Chief of Police; impossible to mistake that face.

'Yes,' the old woman was saying. 'We still 'ave it.'

'Well well!' said Jallen. 'You still have it!'

'Oh yes!' said the old woman – she was about seventy, dressed in very shabby black. 'We still 'ave it up 'ere. Oh yes! Still 'ave our tripe and onions.'

'Would you believe it?' said Jallen. 'Tripe and onions!'

'Tripe an' onions,' she nodded. 'Oh yes! Still 'ave it!'

'These good old English dishes!' enthused Jallen. His attempt at affability and genuine interest was grotesque; incredible that it should fool the woman; but she was obviously a simple old thing, and probably lonely.

'Get the stewpot on!' she quavered. 'That's what my old mother used to say. That's the way to feed a family. Get the stewpot on!'

'The stewpot!' Jallen echoed. 'Makes my mind go back I can tell you. Cold weather and on would go the stewpot. Shin of beef!'

'Oh yes,' the old woman nodded. 'Beef. Bit o' rabbit. Onions.'

'Onions!' said Jallen. 'Ah! Onion stew with beef in it – and rabbit!' He tried – not very successfully – to smack his lips. They weren't the sort of lips that smacked easily, and it would, for that matter, have taken a great actor to have brought mellowness to the metallic voice and warmth to the grim, gashed face.

''Course,' said the old woman, 'shin o' beef was the dearest. Neck o' lamb was cheaper an' just as good. No rabbit in lamb stew. No rabbit. Taters, few leeks, carrots, parsnips, onions –'

'Onions!' Jallen cut in. 'They did it. Flavour! Flavour *and* goodness. But –' he leant forward earnestly – '*tripe* and onions. How do you do it? What's the best way to cook it? I'll bet,' he said confidentially, 'that you know a good old English recipe, one your mother passed on to you from her mother, a sort of –'

Muller, almost subconsciously, had been raising his glass. It slipped and Muller started violently. As the glass rattled to the table Jallen glanced at him. Muller did his best to give an impression of a man who had been drinking and nothing more. He dabbed clumsily at the table and tried to yawn, but he couldn't keep his eyes away from Jallen. He tried, but Jallen was considering him coldly, and Jallen's stare was mesmeric. Best to get up and walk away, Muller told himself, best to stand up in a slightly embarrassed, half-inebriated sort of way, best to . . . but Jallen beat him to it. He strode away, with a last look at Muller and without a word to the old woman.

Muller dabbed his forehead. It was mad, it was incredible. Jallen, a man of immense power and influence, an arch-priest of scientific living and a man who moved in the most select circles, chatting to an impoverished old labouring-class woman in one of the less exclusive housing blocks. Even if the old woman was wanted for something it didn't make sense. Each block was a self-contained community in itself with a resident police force commanded by a chief superintendent. And at H.Q. there was a whole corps of detectives on whom Jallen could call. Besides, there just *wasn't* tripe and onions. Hadn't been for years.

'Tripe and onions,' muttered Muller, walking towards the lifts. It was grotesque; grotesque. And the change in

Jallen's expression when he realized he had been overheard had been remarkable; indeed frightening. Jallen had made his name as a detective, and Muller almost shuddered when he considered what an ordeal it must have been to have been hounded by a man like that. No wonder he had secured a record number of convictions.

There was, of course, only one answer. The old woman must be someone very special, a notorious spy heavily disguised, and Jallen had been playing a cat-and-mouse game with all that talk about defunct recipes. Tripe and onions, Muller muttered, as he stepped towards the magnostrat. Tripe and onions in an age of scientific perfection! Onions were still plentiful, of course, synthetic onions; but no tripe. Definitely no tripe.

*

'I seem to have rung a bell,' said the Superintendent.

Muller's eyes flickered and the Superintendent considered him.

'I've met Jallen,' said Muller, hating the stare. 'What he made of me I don't know, but he certainly baffled me.'

'Oh?'

'He was talking to an old woman about tripe and onions.'

There was a silence.

'Are you trying to be funny?' the Superintendent said softly.

'I am not. It was some time ago. A chance encounter. Jallen was talking to an old woman in Block R. He wanted to know how she cooked tripe and onions. She didn't know who he was and neither did I at first.'

The Superintendent stared for a long time. *'Block R?'* he said at last. *'Tripe and onions?'*

His nose reddened, and Muller laughed. 'You're no more amazed than I was. They were,' he said, 'sitting there drinking in a Bar Annexe. I dropped in by chance for a drink and overheard them talking.'

The Superintendent considered everything carefully.

There might have been maps on every wall of his office and he seemed to be following the outlines of each map.

'Tripe and onions,' he said finally.

'Tripe and onions,' said Muller, 'I've never tasted onions. Tripe, yes.'

'Tripe?' said the Superintendent.

'Many years ago when I was twenty or so. It was in a pub, oddly enough, one of the last of the old pubs. Someone offered me a sandwich of tripe. I didn't like it much.'

'And you remember that?'

'I do.'

The Superintendent took a huge breath and stood up. 'Well. The old woman. Do you know her?'

Muller shook his head.

'Jallen wasn't in uniform?'

'No. But it didn't take me long to recognize him.'

'He certainly has an unforgettable face,' the Superintendent agreed. And he strode up and down. 'What did you make of it?'

'I don't know,' said Muller. 'I could only think she was a spy or something, and that Jallen was trying to catch her out, even though a spy might be expected to know what a police chief looked like. With a face like that, I mean.'

'Yes,' said the Superintendent.

'On the other hand a friend of mine thought the old woman might have something to do with illegal animal breeding. Though how that's possible I don't know.'

The Superintendent was startled; he stared; then he laughed.

'You always seek the clever answer, Muller. I suppose all it amounts to is that some kids at the Higher College of Technology found a way of making tripe. Simple.'

It was Muller's turn to stare.

'Lot of old people in R Block. You know how they talk. "Oh, you should have tasted it, oh the food we used to have. Pig's trotters, jellied eels, tripe". That,' said the Superintendent, 'is how old people talk to their children and grandchildren, and the word would appeal to some of the kids at the Higher Tech. They would muck about and produce tripe.'

He looked well pleased with himself, and Muller had to admit that it was an ingenious explanation.

'Take it to their old granny and say "There you are. Try that and I'll bet you'll find it every bit as good as the tripe you used to have".' The Superintendent laughed. 'Jallen would hear about it, of course. Strictly speaking it would be illegal, very seriously illegal, but I doubt if he'd take action. It's just the sort of thing that would tickle him.'

Muller was surprised, and the Superintendent chuckled. 'You think Jallen pretty frightening. A sort of monster?'

'He looks it,' Muller said briefly. 'And I should have thought his tastes in food were er – elaborate.'

'Yes,' said the Superintendent. 'Oh yes. He's a Block A man all right. Penthouse 2 at that. But he's a surprising man.'

Muller blinked. 'Surprising?'

'What's your image of him?'

Muller shrugged. He didn't know what was in store for him, but for some time he had felt quite calm.

'A repellent man, almost evil, with some degree of cleverness.'

The Superintendent looked at him coolly, then chuckled. 'Cleverer than you, Muller. Jallen's about my age. Fifty-ish. And,' said the Superintendent, 'when Jallen was a young officer there was still a lot of crime about and lawyers and so on, but Jallen was as clever as any lawyer. Never known him worsened by a lawyer. Handsome too. Good-looking in a lean, dark sort of way. He messed up his face in a plane crash.'

'Plane crash?' Muller said politely.

'He's too fond of his Blips. But,' said the Superintendent, 'Jallen as I say was brainy with a hell of a presence and well-spoken into the bargain. Pedigree stock you'd say. Could have married well. But his people were labouring class, always had been, and Jallen married a woman of his own class. Big hefty woman about as pretty as a blob of grease.'

'Interesting,' said Muller.

'Not to me,' the Superintendent demurred. 'I like my women pretty. And,' he said forcefully, 'now that we've let so much hair down I don't mind admitting that I had other preferences. It's going back a long way but Saturday for me meant fishing. That's a long time ago, Muller, and it's not what you'd call a very startling revelation, is it?'

'A very human one,' smiled Muller.

The big man sighed.

'God, how I loved it. Used to belt out to a lake near Wailey and I was so damn keen I couldn't wait to drop my line into the water. Fishing. Remember it, Muller?'

'No.'

'And on the way home there was a beerhouse – I liked your old pubs, make no mistake – a little beerhouse where the ale was served straight from the wood. Marvellous stuff, home-brewed. After a day on the lake and an evening in that pub I felt great. I felt so good I can't put it into words. Not into words,' the Superintendent repeated with emphasis. 'But those were preferences, Muller. You've always dealt in possibilities.'

Muller smiled faintly.

'You can't go back, man,' the Superintendent said with great emphasis. 'You can't go back and you can't beat them. And the point is you see that Jallen has his preferences.'

Muller was startled. 'Don't tell me that *he* yearns for the old way of life?'

The Superintendent smiled.

'I wouldn't put it to the test if I were you. No, Jallen *is* a sort of monster, but he has his lighter side. It used to be girls. Prettier and shapelier they were the better he liked 'em. And it's certainly true that for years Jallen was – girls apart – a sort of machine, inhumanly inflexible, but he's mellowed a lot these last few years. Nothing he likes better than an occasional chat with some nice old party.'

'And . . . tripe?' said Muller.

'Certainly. Maybe it's the family side of him coming out as he gets older, all those generations of peasants and so on. But,' warned the Superintendent, 'these whims of Jallen's are no more than whims. Preferences if you like. And he prefers people who fit neatly into moulds, working-class people particularly.'

'You're warning me?'

'He wouldn't understand you, Muller. He'd have you put down.'

'Some things,' Muller said wearily, 'I find beyond me. The old woman's chat with Jallen still baffles me because she said "We still have it", meaning that they'd never been without it. But words,' said Muller, 'are used loosely, particularly by old people, so there may have been no significance there. You,' Muller said bleakly, 'aren't old; you're big and strong. If people like you had fought for their preferences – decent preferences – Jallen would have been impossible.'

'The big strong man had more sense,' the Superintendent laughed. Then he flushed and snapped angrily: 'Don't be crazy, man. Think of the situation after the nuclear war. Hospitals, churches, schools, factories and for that matter whole damn towns had gone. We had to rebuild and *you* were just a kid then, so it may have seemed one big lark. But to adults the day meant rebuilding and there wasn't time for anything except work.'

'Work,' Muller said tonelessly.

'Yes, work! In the daytime everybody sweated away working like mad. They were too occupied to worry much. But people,' said the Superintendent grimly, '*were* afraid, they were scared stiff.'

'I know,' said Muller.

'And at night' – the Superintendent stood up – 'a lot of them gave way. There were damn-all drugs and that didn't help. It was a sort of tidal wave of hysteria and, for the more phlegmatic types, a terrible sense of desolation, a feeling that nothing was left – no world, no God, no hope.

Every night there were dozens of suicides. Do you,' asked the Superintendent, 'at a time like that think we could have fought for our decent *preferences*?'

His last words flashed out scornfully, and Muller sighed.

'Perhaps not. Not then. But things are a little different now and so am I. I am,' said Muller, 'very much the worse for wear and' – he smiled – 'even in my youth I flung a few hot words about and no more. So why all this talk of Jallen and the police?'

The Superintendent looked at him briefly and sat down.

'You're going to Block Y. Arm T.'

Chapter 2

Block Y was in some ways unusual. Structurally it was – viewed from the front – ordinary enough, the regulation four hundred yards by three hundred of specially treated synthetic concrete, but Block Y, although of standard height, was built in a considerable depression, with the result that the roof – in common with other Blocks the structure was of thirty storeys – was little more than forty feet above ground.

The reason for this was obvious enough. After the nuclear war there were all sorts of experiments and Block Y was the result of one of the earlier theories, that a building erected below ground level wouldn't be seriously damaged by blast. Experiments had complicated this theory. Using a similar building and nuclear devices scientists had discovered that although blast wouldn't – as with more orthodox erections – slice it from the face of the earth it could be equally damaging. Although the structure might escape completely, freaks of blast – cross-blast from the larger bombs – could whip it (underground shelters and all) from its hole like a cork blown from a bottle, with disastrous results.

With human life more important now than buildings, structures on the lines of Block Y were obviously undesirable. Although the more orthodox housing blocks were built above ground their enormously deep shelters were impregnable against anything except direct hits. Even now the odd rocket could be embarrassing, but for long it had been the policy to abandon any town severely damaged, and this presented few problems. Scattered about the country were many ghost towns, each town consisting of ten or twenty blocks, and the erection and renewal of such towns was quite simple now that building technique was so advanced. The blocks were fully equipped and entirely self-contained, even to the industrial and sewage gasification units on the lower floors, and it was, therefore, a simple matter for the survivors of shattered towns to transfer to a ghost town. When, for instance, Northampton was destroyed the survivors moved to N1; with the destruction of N1 they moved to N2; when N2 was hit they moved to N3, and so on.

It was a simple process, marred only by the unfortunate incident when Northampton was struck for the fourth time and Coventry for the seventeenth. Due to confusion at higher levels the Northampton people were moved to C18 and the Coventry people to N5. C18 was, of course, a twenty-block town, twice the size of N5, and initial doubt caused an overwrought Northampton official to phone the Regional Director's Office.

'C-C18,' he began nervously, 'C-C18,' and a metallic voice told him he'd see nineteen if he didn't explain himself, and quickly. 'The towns have crossed,' the official shrieked hysterically. 'This is Corthamptry. That's where we should be but the switchovers got crossed. The b's must be there and here we are at their place. Where? 18, you fool, there's a damn great C right in front of me now.'

Blips shrieked into the air and police cars roared down the magnostrat.

*

But Block Y was fortunate in not being hit directly, and in miraculously surviving all blasts and cross-blasts. It was, therefore, allowed to stand, particularly as its largely subterranean construction appealed to various authorities. Constructionally steps were taken to obviate any risk, shafts being bored far below the bottom storey, leading to tunnels with linking passages, and safety outlets well away from Block Y.

There were the obvious uses, storage and experiments of one sort and another, but superstition dies hard, and, as

Block Y emerged unscathed from the haphazard attacks that followed the nuclear war, it acquired the reputation of a 'lucky' building. And thus some higher officials with suites in the glittering Hall of Administration found various reasons for taking root in the gloomier depths of Block Y. This was scarcely necessary, since Wapsaw as a whole had been extraordinarily fortunate, it being one of the few towns in the country to retain its original position. ('Wars have come and wars have gone, but Wapsaw's soil is still its own', as the schoolchildren sang, not entirely logically.)

Gossip was inevitable, for Block Y was controlled directly by the police, and was retained primarily to house the lower order of manual workers and the town's more dubious citizens, its two hundred-odd prostitutes included, but the latter couldn't be visited without a permit, and the Chief Sanitary Inspector – one of those who had chosen to burrow deeply into Block Y – answered one sly wink and a leering 'Any luck today, old cock?' with, 'No, Dick. You try dipping your wick without a chit from Bob Block.'

Inspector Block, of course, was a pillar of the new order, and was notoriously unbending.

*

With the change in scientific opinion the approaches to the building were altered. Block Y initially with its front entrance almost a hundred yards below ground level could be approached only by lift. The sides of the vast well in which the building nestled were perpendicular, but a row of lifts three hundred yards away led to mechanical pavements that moved smoothly to (and from) the front entrance. All this had now been scrapped; a channel had been blasted through the concrete and a road swooped down to the front doors.

The change, although desirable, had the effect of making the approach to the building somewhat unpleasant; it was like arriving abruptly at a fortress, an impression that wasn't lessened by the considerable body of police always in evidence; but the only thing odd about the structure wasn't at the front or the sides but at the rear. Not that anyone was likely to approach the rear of the building, but more than one police recruit drilling out on the square had glanced up at the glass attachments sticking out from the rear of the building.

There were twenty or thirty of them, and, from a hundred yards or so, they seemed fragile, pipe-like things prodding out from the huge bulk of the main structure, but each of them measured about twenty-five feet by twelve, and they were so elevated and angled – set at different heights and angles – that each could be observed without confusion or error of identity. One couldn't obscure another. It didn't take long for the rawest recruit to the paramilitary Mobile Police to learn that the glass attachments were flats, most of them occupied by men, but some by women. It was, morever, possible to look down into the flats from the roof of the buildings and to look up into them from the ground. They could for that matter be viewed from all angles, and with clarity, because all the furnishings of the flats were transparent, and floodlights played their part at night.

As bedtime approached men (not all of them recruits) lined the low parapet of the roof and stared down at the flats, the occupants of which had to conform to a code of behaviour. This was simple enough and included rules of personal hygiene and undressing before going to bed. New arrivals particularly were inclined to be impressionable, and modest, and when they saw men staring down at them from what seemed (and in some cases was) only a few feet they panicked; jumped into bed fully clothed or had hysterics, or both. The watchers on the roof, of course, reported this and the delinquents were dealt with at once. The modest were (after two warnings) given the tapthyneurogalz treatment, and this, as some of the prostitutes could testify, had side effects. 'Not,' as Inspector Block said to the Chief Sanitary Inspector, 'that I would call them side effects.'

Chapter 3

Muller was drunk. Mildly but sufficiently drunk in the Bar 1 Annexe at Block R. Dreamily he pressed a coin downwards and magically the foaming glass drifted upwards. Hazily he reflected that progress had its compensation; in the days when drink was served at bars some men had enjoyed fighting (as they put it in Wapsaw; notoriously a town of heavy drinkers) for drinks at bars, but how very much pleasanter, Muller pondered, to sit down at a table, dial a letter, and watch the glass sighing upwards in the latticed metal cup. Even the hole in the table wasn't an eyesore or a pitfall: a touch of the finger and a cover concealed it. ('And I have known them who've spewed into it,' Mr Andrews had laughed.)

It was true, of course, true, that the dialling (B for bitter, C for cider, D for draught beer) could be risky, particularly if one was hazy or drunk, but the electronic brain that supervised the apparatus was marvellous, and if, for instance, one inserted a florin and dialled for a whisky there was a shriek from a buzzer and a reminder that a whisky was three shillings. That, of course, was simple enough; another shilling had to be inserted; but cider was a shilling, a brown ale (BA) cost threepence more and a pale ale (PA) sixpence more; confusion, Muller found, came with the simpler things. Draught ale (D) was one-and-threepence a pint, best draught (BD) was one-and-fourpence; bitter (B) was one-and-fivepence and best bitter (BB) was one-and-ninepence.

To begin with Muller – in a state of high tension – had inserted one-and-six and dialled BBB. The electronic brain (thinking he wanted best bitter) had demanded another threepence, but Muller's fumbling hand couldn't find a threepenny bit, so he rammed sixpence into the slot and dialled BBBB, hoping by emphasis (B for bitter) to make things clear, but a tart voice had asked him for clarification. 'Bitter!' Muller had bawled. 'Bitter!' In his confusion he didn't realize that the thing couldn't hear him, but a nice old man (it was morning and very few people were in the room) from a near by table came to his assistance, remarking that these things were all right when you knew how to use them. 'I don't drink much,' said Muller, emptying the pint in two gulps.

He sank a second pint almost as quickly, and for a moment thought he would be sick. He retched violently, then his stomach settled and he felt better. The old man was staring at him unblinkingly, so he changed his position and (knowing he shouldn't – the muck would give him a headache) drank a third pint, and felt beautifully calm and hazy. He sat awhile in a sort of trance, then it occurred to him that not everybody drank pints. After staring at the dial and finding no half-pint indicator he stood up, standing quite still for two or three minutes because the blood was pounding in his head, then he sat down again shakily, realizing that he hadn't been standing as steadily as all that.

'You all right?' asked the old man, coming up.

'Touch of blood pressure, I think,' said Muller. 'Head like an old engine pounding away.'

'It's blood pressure all right,' nodded the old man. 'You want to take it easy.'

'Can't,' said Muller. 'I'm a desperate character.'

The old man laughed.

'Truth,' said Muller. 'I'm being transferred to the star dungeon at Block Y.'

'You're a comic,' chuckled the old man. 'But you don't look well. Take my tip an' go easy on this muck. It's no good for blood pressure.'

He was walking away smiling when Muller called him back.

'Can you get a half out of this thing?'

'Course you can,' said the old man. 'You put your money in an' set this little arrow thing on this mark 'ere.'

'Damned if I can see it,' said Muller.

'Nothin' to it,' said the old man. 'Do you know where they had all this tomfool idea from?'

Muller shook his head.

'I'll tell you,' said the old man. 'Dairies. Fillin' bottles of milk in dairies.'

'Dairies?'

'Bottlin' milk. Wonderful machinery they had.'

'Did you work in a dairy?'

'I did that. Thirty years I was in a dairy. Fine healthy job too.'

'Pleasant sort of job,' said Muller.

'Marvellous,' enthused the old man. 'Built me up as you might say. 'Course,' he added, 'that was in the days when we 'ad milk.'

Muller sighed. He felt sober again but another quick pint restored his tranquillity. He sat for quite a time and when he looked up he was alone. The old man must have gone to lunch. Muller smiled as he thought of the tripe and onions, then melancholy settled on him again, and he counted his change. 'Oh, damn it!' he told himself, 'meeting the van was as bad as entering hospital for a major operation.' He downed another pint and felt quite drunk.

Forty-five minutes to go. He thought of a story he had read years ago. It was set in the tropics and Muller remembered few details but it was about a man who had gone native. An old friend looked him up and found him in a bad way. He had taken to drugs and his native woman supplied him with his daily quota. There wasn't much else to it and it wasn't important. As the friend walked away he asked himself what the end would be. Not a very original observation: 'I wondered what the end would be': but it had stuck in Muller's mind because his own life had been so very uncertain.

'I wondered what the end would be.' Many times over the last few years the phrase had echoed in Muller's mind. There was one thing. In the old days people could take a taxi or bus or car, they could take a train and plane or ship and head for Ireland or America or anywhere in the world. In Britain and Europe there were tens of thousands of cities and towns and villages that might give refuge, innumerable hamlets and hostels and even monasteries that could provide sanctuary, but all that was gone. There was no escape. Travel abroad was unknown. There were no taxis, no trains, no ships and no planes for civilian use. Only four coastal resorts remained, and people travelled to (if they had a permit) and from them by car or bus, but the cars and buses were held to the magnostrat by the apparatus that powered them. Away from it they were as impotent as a trolley-bus divorced from its power cable had been. Only police and military (and some official) cars had independent power units.

And so and so, Muller asked himself. So what? He didn't know. One thing was certain. He had a cheque due on Friday and this was Tuesday or Wednesday, and he had damn-all money. He started to count it, but gave up because there were too many pennies and ha'pennies, and the whole blasted lot amounted to only a few shillings. Eight maybe. They haven't managed to do away with money, Muller muttered, counting out six pennies and another two pennies and a half-penny. One by one they dropped into the slot, then Muller, growling contemptuously, moved the tiny arrow to the microscopic ½ sign, and dialled B. The dial didn't swing round to its full extent, so he dialled B again, and the voice promptly demanded another twopence. 'You crazy bastards!' snarled Muller. 'You barmy gimcrack bastards!' In rapid succession he dialled A, AB, BB, BBC, CA, PA, BD, PA and BO: the voice shrieked in alarm and a severe-looking gentleman appeared at Muller's elbow.

He looked like a floorwalker but he was the area assistant manager.

'And what,' he demanded, 'is the big idea?'

Muller nearly flashed at him but he stopped himself just in time.

'We have ways,' snapped the A.A.M., 'of handling drunken louts.'

Muller grinned sheepishly.

'Even reforming them,' continued the A.A.M.

Muller's grin faded. He felt sick, tired; but full of hate.

'I wish,' he sighed . . .

'Wish what?' snapped the A.A.M.

'Wish,' said Muller . . . 'Wish. Oh . . . wish I could sit in a cosy room. Press a bell and have a drink brought to me.'

'A very human wish,' agreed the A.A.M. 'And one that could be gratified if you lived in Block A or Block B. But,' said the A.A.M. severely, 'you have to be a person of brains or quality to live in Block A or Block B, not a working-class lout. Brains and quality, my friend. As it is I'll have your name and number and withdraw your permit for a month.'

'Permit?' said Muller.

'Certainly, permit. For a month – no, three months – you'll be barred from the Hall of Pleasure.'

'There's much I could say,' sighed Muller.

'There is, eh?'

'Particularly about the tripe and onions.'

The A.A.M. almost jumped.

'Tripe and onions!'

'But we'll let it pass. The decision, if you knew it, is irrevocable. I am,' said Muller, 'barred. As of today.'

*

'You're going to Block Y. Arm T,' the Estate Superintendent had said, and Muller had paled. When he lit a cigarette his hand was trembling. Very briefly the Superintendent's face softened with compassion. Then it was wiped away, to be replaced with a mask of professional hardness.

'It's not so bad. Take it easy, Muller.'

'Not so bad,' Muller said hoarsely. 'I suppose not. Nothing ever is.'

'Of course not.'

'Didn't someone last nine months there once?'

The Superintendent laughed.

'The record. Isn't the usual time two or three days?'

'Nonsense,' the Superintendent said blandly. 'The remedial extensions have done good work.'

'Particularly with the girls who've been turned into prostitutes. They've been extended all right.' Muller's hand was still shaking a little. There wasn't an ashtray. He looked round jerkily and the Superintendent got up quickly and took the cigarette from him.

'Didn't know you were interested in prostitutes, Muller.'

'I'm not.' His mouth was horribly dry. 'Not the type.'

'Neither am I,' the Superintendent said soothingly. 'I'm old-fashioned I know, but I doubt if I've had more than six or seven women in my life.' He stared steadily at Muller. 'Pity you never married.'

'Yes.'

'Why not?'

Muller shrugged. 'Until I was twenty-seven or so I didn't bother. Then I did bother, very much, but it was no good. As you've pointed out I'm not much of a capture.'

The Superintendent took a long, slow breath, warmly and gently, like a man remembering a splendid meal. 'Pity. I like women. In the best sort of way, I mean. Makes life more attractive just having them around.'

'Plenty around here,' Muller said gloomily.

'Certainly. Quite a few unmarried. Nice girls too. Pretty. Good figures. Thoroughly trained. They would,' the Superintendent said softly, 'be pleasurable in bed and they'd be more than adequate domestically. Make good wives. What more can a man want if he has a decent job and so on?'

Muller shrugged. 'Depends I suppose.'

'But,' the Superintendent said more briskly, 'I

wouldn't worry about prostitutes if I were you. Girls only become prostitutes because they're too idle for ordinary work.'

'Prostitutes be damned,' snapped Muller. 'I never give them a thought.' He felt steadier but his face was burning.

'Muller,' said the Superintendent, 'this is one of the last contacts you'll have with the outside world. For a long time you won't be allowed to leave Block Y. And if you want to live and have any chance at all you'll have to change. You'll have to do what you haven't done before. And that is keep a level head. Keep your emotions under control.'

There was a long silence.

'Personally I think you're harmless. It's the order of the Committee that you be sent to Block Y and there's not much I can do about it. But Muller' – the big man's voice was quite gentle – 'try to adapt yourself. Try to behave. The time will soon pass. It always does. Retirement age normally is sixty and although circumstances aren't normal I'll make a strong recommendation that at fifty you be transferred to a Home of Rest.'

Muller stared. His heart seemed to be strangling him.

'Take it easy,' the Superintendent said quietly.

Muller tried to speak. He couldn't. Not for two or three minutes. Then – his voice shrill and discordant – he said: 'Only twenty or so years to go! Do you think I'll last?'

'No,' the Superintendent said sombrely. 'I don't.'

'Well!' Muller laughed shrilly. 'Love and marriage and the nice girls in the office and off you go to the torture chamber. All within a few minutes!'

'It's your only chance,' said the Superintendent.

'Only chance! What do you mean?'

The Superintendent stood up and stared bleakly.

'I mean that in the strange times in which we live almost anything can happen. You could be killed by bombing. So could I. So could the Committee. More prosaically some members of the Committee come up for re-election in two years' time and they might lose their seats. It is,' the Superintendent said carefully, 'a possibility. In that event I'd bring your name forward and you might be released. You might be. And' – his voice was louder and just faintly sarcastic – 'if you last two years in Block Y you'll have a damn sight more sense than you've got now. You'll smarten yourself up. Get a decent, ordinary sort of a job. The nice girl and so on will soon follow.'

Muller stared. Was the Superintendent hinting that there might be a change in the balance of power, a struggle behind the scenes or an open revolt, and that he – this big man who looked the part, this important man who was going out of his way to –

'Hope,' the Superintendent said sharply. 'There's always hope.'

They began to walk towards the door.

'What would you do if you were in my position?' asked Muller.

'The van,' said the Superintendent, 'will call for you at 2 p.m. tomorrow. If you have killed yourself it will remove your body.'

'Thanks,' Muller said grimly.

'You'll be allowed to take only your personal things. Take your writing too. But not if it's harmful.'

In the passage that led to the outer door they paused.

'If I went against authority I'd go all the way,' said the Superintendent. 'If I failed my position would be hopeless. In that event I'd put a pistol to my head.'

Muller stared. 'Pistol to your head! What a curiously old-fashioned phrase!'

'I'm a curiously old-fashioned man,' retorted the Superintendent, smiling grimly. 'I'm all for progress and the scientific way of life. But every man should have the right to go fishing. Good-bye, Muller.'

Chapter 4

The driver of the big black van was lean and grim but the two constables who came to the door were fat and cheerful. They looked so human that Muller lost some of his sick dread, and felt better.

'Ready?' grinned one, and Muller pointed to the one small case and the huge cardboard box. The latter was many years old – it had stood up in the loft for half a lifetime – and one of the constables kicked it and asked what it was.

'Papers,' Muller said nervously. 'Old manuscripts and whatnot. I was told to take them.'

'Right,' said the constable, and with an easy swing hoisted the box to his shoulder.

Muller looked back into the living room, and the van driver – much older than his comrades – walked up.

'This is a house, Smithy,' grinned the young man holding the case. 'Ever been in a house before, Smithy?'

The driver stared into the room, at the shabby furniture and the one comfortable armchair, at the fading flowers in a vase and the three pictures of Muller's parents. 'Lived in one once,' he said flatly.

'He lived in one once,' grinned the constable with the bag. 'Did you like it, Smithy?'

'I did,' the driver said expressionlessly.

'W-what,' Muller stammered, 'what's it like in Y Block?' It was a stupid question and he despised himself for asking it, hated himself for being afraid, and (most frightening of all) found himself all the more uncertain because these men had a sort of authority, almost a *rightness*, that made him feel culpable and (even worse) helpless.

'You must fight,' he told himself. '*Fight,*' but the young men grinned, and the one with the box on his shoulder chuckled: 'Like! You don't know what *you've* been missing!'

'Wait till you see the girls,' grinned the second young man. 'You'll be able to sit there or just lie in bed and –'

'That's no way to speak to a detainee,' the driver broke in sharply, and there was a silence, the one young man grinning sheepishly and the other scowling a little. 'Only trying to cheer the poor little sod up,' grumbled the latter. 'What have you done anyway, mate?'

'*Mate!*' thought Muller. So human, so unexpectedly human. 'Done?' he said. 'Nothing. I've lived here all my life. But these houses are coming down so I have to be rehoused. And they've gone over my old books and found something they don't like.'

'*Books?*' said the driver.

'Novels,' explained Muller. 'Stories.'

They stared.

'Stories,' said Muller. 'You know – tales about – about love and adventure and things like that.'

They still seemed doubtful, but the more independent of the young constables said: 'You've got to be rehoused so they're moving you to the Zoo . . . the special whatsits?'

Muller nodded.

'If they'd left these houses alone you'd have been O.K.?'

Again Muller nodded and the constable whistled. 'Christ!' He stared at Muller, then turned to the driver. 'How's that for luck, Smithy?'

The driver pawed the floor. 'Too bad. But some of these writers . . . they have theories an' that. Come on. We'd better be going.'

Muller had said nothing to the neighbours. Only two of them saw him go. Forty years he'd been in the street, and he wasn't sentimental about it because there wasn't much to be sentimental about. The house was different, it was home, or had been home, it was the home his parents had made, and the home that he had (when they were alive) taken for granted. But the greatest upheaval of his life had been the loss of his father and mother, and although he had – slowly and painfully – got over it, the house not only acquired all sorts of meanings; in many ways it haunted him. It was too full of memories; if it had been possible he would have moved. But the days had passed when one could take another house or flat or just ... go away. One could, of course (subject to approval), stay with relatives, if one had relatives, and if they lived in the same town, and there were, of course, State convalescent centres and the like for duly approved persons, but the one certain way to move was to die. There had over the years been quite a few deaths in the street, and the bodies had been taken to the crematorium with dispatch and with as little ceremony as Muller was being removed now. He wondered if his fate was to be similar.

But the policeman had – oddly and surprisingly – cheered and encouraged him. Muller recognized that they were labourers and not the artisans of Jallen's Special Branch, but they *were* policemen, fully trained and indoctrinated; the two young men, for all that, not only seemed *more* human than most ordinary people, the driver (a man verging on middle age) had something about him that suggested dissatisfaction with things as they were. Lack of promotion, perhaps. But there seemed soil here that a man like the Superintendent could cultivate.

For ten minutes the engine whined steadily, then the van dipped so abruptly that Muller was flung forward. The door opened and Muller climbed out. He had a fleeting (and frightening) impression of standing at the bottom of a great gorge with an immense building towering over him, then the (so jovial and understanding) young policemen grabbed him and marched him quickly into the building. It hurt; each held an arm in a crudely applied lock, and Muller – pained and surprised – gasped, 'Ease up; there's no need for this,' but they hustled him along the great hall, through doors that seemed to open magically, along passages, across an ante-room full of policemen, one of whom opened a door inscribed 'Chief Inspector Veale'.

*

It was a large, white room sparsely equipped. At a small desk sat a policewoman. She was about twenty-five, very dark and pretty. At right angles to the small desk was a larger desk but the man behind it made it less than executive-sized. He was fiftyish, with a large fat face and big grey eyes. His face was smooth and pale, and he was fat; his belly seemed to start at his chest and arc outwards from there.

The policemen released Muller and saluted. 'The detainee, Muller, Sir,' one of them said, and the fat inspector stared for a full minute, then nodded. The constables saluted again, and withdrew.

The inspector seemed to be considering something, and the effort was tiring. His breathing was laboured, as though he had been drinking. At last he held out a fat hand, and the girl pushed Muller's dossier into it. The inspector let his huge eyes rest on it for two or three minutes, then he closed it, sighing heavily.

'My liver, Mr Muller, is giving me hell,' he said. His voice was heavy and laboured, but curiously lifeless. For a moment or so his chest went up and down, his great cod-eyes glazed but apprehensive, then he wheezed: 'Politics. Good for letting off steam. Pity they're not fashionable.'

Muller, who had been trembling with hurt and anger, then standing shakily on one leg and the other, was surprised. 'Politics,' he said. 'I've never had much to do with politics.'

The inspector waved a fat hand.

'You make the bullets. Other people fire them. The bullets have to be made.'

'But I've never fed people with propaganda,' Muller protested. 'I've never been active in anything like that.'

The inspector waved breathlessly. 'You produce ideas – ideas that aren't liked.'

'Heavens above,' said Muller, 'I know what I like and know what I dislike, and I've said so – years ago, when people could express their feelings.'

'Ah,' the inspector breathed sadly. 'You know the unwritten law. You like what you're supposed to like.'

Muller gestured angrily, and the inspector released hot air in a protracted sigh.

'My job,' he said, 'is the extermination of rubbish.'

Muller flushed.

'Which,' said the inspector, 'is odd seeing that my own drainage system is faulty.' He breathed heavily. 'Forty years ago I would have retired on pension. Bred Sealyham terriers or something like that.'

'Don't policemen still retire on pension?' asked Muller.

'They do. And most of them younger and fitter than I.' The inspector seemed to ponder on that, looking almost comically like an alcoholic on a remorseful morning-after. 'Of course,' he breathed, rousing himself, 'it would be easy to say that I'm so devoted to the new order – perfection, scientific and human – that I prefer to conceal my condition.'

Muller groped for a chair and – to his surprise – saw that the pretty police girl had gone. The inspector must have sent her out at the beginning of the interview.

'And,' the inspector continued, taking an enormous breath, 'that would be true to some extent. But concealment isn't always easy.'

Muller shook suddenly and laughed.

'Congratulations,' said the inspector. 'You're the first man to come here and laugh.'

'Hysterical laughter probably,' said Muller.

'Probably. But as I was trying to say . . . logic's an odd thing. The genius,' said the inspector, expelling then gathering breath, 'who first thought of the remedial extensions had the idea that the greatest fear of criminal-subversive types was being seen. Some of them, of course, glory in it.'

'For long?' asked Muller.

'Well,' said the inspector, 'I said my job was to exterminate rubbish, but you, for instance, are not a plain thief. You're not easily classified.' He pondered on that, breathing heavily. 'This is a place of torture but there's more to it than that. We contribute to medical science and we do quite a few reconversion jobs.'

'Reconversion?' Muller said jerkily.

'You know,' said the inspector, snoring in air, 'what scientists are. In the name of research they're often nasty little boys. But with ordinary people – I mean the middle-class authoritarian type – it's a bit of a nuisance. Research workers,' he panted, 'are so dedicated. Beautifully simple. You give 'em bodies and whatnot to play about with and they're happy.'

Muller didn't know what to make of this man, but he realized that he wasn't necessarily less to be feared than the type of official traditionally feared: lean, grim, peaked cap low over eyes.

'And the ruling middle classes,' he said. 'What do they want?'

The fat inspector chuckled, and this brought on a spell of breathlessness that silenced him for two or three minutes. His huge eyes glassy and downcast, he fell into a reverie, apparently contemplating his own fate.

'Well,' he resumed at last, 'well; now what did such people do years ago? They had all sorts of interests. They went abroad. They went motoring. Yachting. They played golf. Activities that interested them, passed the time, and took care of any surplus energy. Now all that's gone.'

'And everybody's happy,' said Muller.

'Sensible,' retorted the inspector. 'They don't come *here*. But,' he said, 'ours is an indoor civilization and man is a sexual animal. So there you are; more bodies.'

'Satisfy them sexually,' murmured Muller. 'Prostitutes galore.'

The inspector laughed and became breathless again.

'You're an idiot,' he wheezed. 'We cater for the elite.

How many men in this town matter? At rock bottom two or three. With twenty or thirty close to them and three hundred worthy of account. Four hundred all together say, but subtract those who are . . . content. That leaves us with two hundred or so.'

'Two hundred,' echoed Muller.

The inspector breathed gustily and spread his great paws. 'It always amazes me.'

'What does?'

'Sex. So old. Oldest thing in the world.' The inspector sighed, for a moment appearing to shrink from a sad mountain of a man to a soggy balloon. 'Personally I've never been that way inclined.'

'Neither have I,' said Muller.

'Not inclined?'

'Oh yes. Very much so I suppose.' Muller shrugged. 'But I've never met the woman I'd like to meet.'

The inspector shook.

'All right,' said Muller. 'I'm not much good at it.'

The inspector breathed gustily. 'With me it's a matter of temperament. Must be. With the measures available here I could be as virile as ten niggers, but there you are.'

'Measures?' said Muller.

'Operational.'

'Why,' asked Muller, 'don't you have an operation on your liver?'

'Have had,' breathed the inspector. 'Don't know what they did to it, but my kidney's not my own.'

'Doesn't seem to add up to scientific perfection,' suggested Muller.

'That's the hell of it,' sighed the inspector. 'The operation *is* successful. Invariably.'

'You're a sort of odd man out?'

'I suppose so. Not an enviable position as you know. But,' breathed the inspector, 'my customers – the men we're talking about – are not; they're not odd men out. They're what I call S-men. Full of drive and energy, too busy being busy to doubt the oligarchy they adorn. Couldn't doubt it anyway, they're not that type, but definitely something extra about them – personality and so on – that makes their success understandable and inevitable.'

'Are you speaking generally?' asked Muller.

The inspector, recapturing his breath, didn't answer for two or three minutes.

'You're referring to our rulers?' said Muller.

'I am. And you know it. And,' said the inspector, 'there is something superior about them, if only physically. They stand out. I don't mean because they're giants or perfect specimens – most of them aren't; but there is something naturally authoritative about them. Commanding. And there you are.'

'There we are what?' asked Muller.

The inspector began to shake again, but became breathless.

'Never mind,' he wheezed.

Muller's mind returned to his interview with the Estate Superintendent. Hadn't he said that Jallen had been fond of the girls, the shapelier and prettier the better? It was quite possible that Jallen had started all this business.

'Such men,' said the inspector, as one talking to a simpleton, 'take some satisfying. They're often highly sexed and because of their thrustfulness – or whatever it is – they're successful early in life. Successful sexually, I mean. Then in the natural order of things they enjoy the services of attractive wives and secretaries and so on. When they're bored with all that they come to me.'

'It must be a problem,' said Muller.

'Problem!' exclaimed the inspector feelingly. 'It's a nightmare!' He shook his head and sighed.

'What do you do?' asked Muller. 'Sort of classify them according to age and so on?'

'I try,' said the inspector, 'but you know how it is with people of influence. Never satisfied.' He took a huge breath.

'Generally speaking, of course, they require more subtlety as they get older.'

'I suppose so,' Muller murmured gravely.

'Simple things – Chinese massage and so on – are all very well to start with.'

'Chinese massage?'

'It may not be Chinese but I think the blind prostitutes of China specialized in it.'

'*Blind* prostitutes?'

'They were naturally blind some of them. Trained, of course, from childhood. Their blindness gave them great delicacy of touch.'

'Are your prostitutes . . . blind?' asked Muller.

'They're beautiful,' the inspector said blandly. 'Chinese massage by a couple of girls – I use them in pairs, naked of course – isn't bad to start with.'

'Erotic,' said Muller.

'Very. But you know what people are. They like a performance.'

'Gladiators. Bear baiting. Pretty girls.'

'You understand,' said the inspector. His breathing seemed to be easier. 'A pity,' he said, 'your life has moved on the wrong lines. You might have helped me in my work.'

'Must be fascinating,' said Muller.

'It is. It is. But you can still help me.'

'Oh? How?'

'It is,' said the inspector, 'a good thing to kill two birds with one stone. It's even better to kill two hundred and two birds with one stone.' He spread his hands. 'It's a thing the artist in you will appreciate. To put on a show that will arouse the enthusiasm of the under-thirties and at the same time interest the more er – experienced tastes of the over-fifties.'

'A tall order,' said Muller.

'Quite. But just occasionally I can pull it off. Just occasionally. Top of the bill next Saturday will be you and Kitty One-Eye.'

Muller had felt stultified; emotionally almost dissociated, as though listening to other men talking. Now he felt the first twinges of fear.

'Kitty One-Eye?'

'You don't know her?' The inspector chuckled when Muller didn't answer, and stared fixedly until Muller said hotly: 'Terrible though my sins are I've had a very restricted life. I know few people and I've never heard of Kitty One-Eye.'

The inspector cluck-clucked. 'Quite. Well, the amazing thing about Kitty is the fact that she's alive. She has the most obscene tongue of anyone I've known – man or woman – and she's been a public nuisance for longer than I can remember.'

Muller stared.

'She's small and thin. Carrotty-haired but she's a bit grey now. You don't know her?'

'I've told you I don't know her,' Muller said angrily.

'You've written some pretty hot stuff in your time.'

'I know.'

'Didn't it interest women?'

'I had shoals of letters.'

'And chose freedom?'

'I was a poor performer but good at writing about it.'

'With Kitty,' said the inspector, 'I'm sure it was the other way about. Not that she didn't inspire poetry of course.' And with a suitably solemn air he intoned:

'O Wapsaw! noble on the Tame!
O splendid city, fair and free!
My dick is somehow not the same
Since One-Eyed Kate enraptured me!'

Muller, staring fixedly, laughed once, and the inspector sighed.

'Those chants of one's schooldays.' He sighed again, then – more briskly – said: 'Kitty took to prostitution in her teens. She was very good at it, I understand, but she also took to drink. What with that and her temper and her foul mouth she was often in trouble. Generations of policemen have known her. She had served quite a few terms for drunk and disorderly before I was born.'

'*Before* –' Muller began, and the inspector laughed, his cheeks shaking.

'I'm fifty-three and Kitty's well over seventy. But she's as spry as a chicken – or as a chicken used to be.'

Muller stared, and the inspector laughed again – silently – and went on: 'Kitty started with a good class of client but she was down to entertaining labourers by the time she was thirty. She was a bit light-fingered and that didn't help. She took many a bashing and one man put her eye out. At forty she looked vile; at fifty grotesque.'

The inspector took a huge breath and sighed gustily. 'No man would look at her, of course. She made a living – if it can be called that – hawking shoelaces round drinking halls. When they didn't buy or give her a few coppers she insulted them. And to be insulted by Kitty was something.'

There was a long silence. 'The lesson,' said the inspector, 'if it is a lesson, is applicable to you. Kitty offended, outraged and disgusted people. She'd have been sent down for years – or when the new order came in put down for good – but she got away with it because she was comic. She has the vilest mouth of anyone I've known – the most obscene and blasphemous – but also the most amusing. She's a scream.'

Muller stared tensely.

'For some years now she's been a bit potty. Nothing serious. Delusions of wealth and so on. Physically she's a marvel – as active as a thirty-year-old. But some weeks ago she had trouble with a foot – a touch of gangrene or something – and they amputated three toes. As you can imagine' – the inspector chuckled – 'she was a bit too much for our young nurses, so we brought her here. She is now on her feet – or foot – again, and more horribly funny than ever.'

Muller thought for a moment. 'And the performance?'

'Just remove your clothes, will you?'

'Remove . . . ?'

'Your clothes. Strip. You have to be medically examined.'

Muller looked slowly round the office. There were no facilities for medical examination. But yards away were dozens of policemen. The inspector had only to press a bell.

'That's right, Muller. I can't retire. I know so much that I'm almost indispensable. That may be a word for it but they prefer to keep me well in view. In short I have to go on working and die with my boots on. I advise you to remove yours.'

Muller undressed. When he was down to his pants the police girl came in. He hesitated, then caught the inspector's eye. Muller turned his back to the girl and removed his pants.

'Good.' The inspector got up and approached Muller. Now that he was on his feet he looked enormous. 'Good. Not well-endowed by nature but that can't be helped.' The inspector's breathing was heavy and noisy again. 'H'm.' Gently he patted Muller's slightly protuberant stomach. 'Too much pie, Muller, too much pie.'

Muller, scarcely breathing, held himself rigidly.

'Dear me,' sighed the inspector, 'no wonder you're not married. You couldn't make many girls young mothers with *that*.' His immense hand engulfed Muller's penis and gave it a playful tug. 'What one might call buried treasure,' breathed the inspector. 'Not easy to find. Almost a secret weapon, in fact.'

Muller burned with shame and anger. Playfully the inspector turned him towards the girl. Muller jerked away and the inspector hit him with the flat of his hand. Muller went down, his head crashing into the girl's desk.

He felt sick when he got up and his head was ringing. The inspector – seated again – replaced the telephone and cluck-clucked.

'Did I hurt you? I didn't mean to. It's this confounded weight of mine. A playful tap I assure you.'

Muller glanced at the police girl. Her face was a little red and she was staring intently at a paper on her desk.

'But let it be a lesson to you. Implicit obedience and submission is the only sensible thing in a place like this.'

A thin, gloomy man came in followed by two attendants in white coats.

'Ah!' said the inspector. 'Doctor Fallow. Don't stop to knock.'

The doctor stared sourly at Muller. 'What's this?'

'Detainee. One James Muller. Working-class writer. Reactionary. Violently opinionated and rebelliously inclined.'

'Never heard of him.'

'He's led a restricted life. But he has to be examined.'

The doctor examined Muller. It was a perfunctory examination and was soon over.

'Any use to you?'

The doctor snorted disgustedly. 'Good God no! Sedentary going-to-seed type. We had hundreds like him to begin with. Could do with a few husky young brutes now.'

'Quite. In the interests of patriotism and research I do think a few might volunteer. Perhaps they will. But –' the inspector was almost purring – 'it's a dull season and there's not much on next Saturday. I thought we might have an engagement between our friend here and Kitty One-Eye.'

'Engagement?'

'A love bout. Copulation. An hour's frenzied intercourse.'

The doctor's eyes gleamed a little. 'You old devil. But it could be interesting.'

'Interesting! Kate should be worth going a long way to hear!'

'A collector's item,' the doctor said dryly. 'But' – he glanced at Muller – 'he's not very well equipped.'

'He'll respond to treatment surely?'

The doctor shrugged. 'Perhaps. Partially.'

'Come now doctor,' the inspector said smoothly. 'I think you have drugs in mind. I didn't ask for them when I called you.'

'I didn't answer the phone,' the doctor snapped. 'And there isn't time for an operation.'

'Exactly. That is a point of course. But it had occurred to me.'

'Oh all right,' the doctor said testily, and one of the attendants stepped forward, and placed a case on the inspector's desk.

Muller moved once and the attendants held his arms as the doctor fastened a belt around him, just above his hips. It was of webbing material and there were pads that fitted firmly around the base of Muller's penis. There were two underbelts; as the doctor clipped them to the belt Muller's inside seemed to rise, as though he was sinking rapidly in a half-speed lift.

'Observe, my dear Muller,' the inspector almost cooed, 'how we progress. It's always been done, of course, but the ancients were incredible. In Africa they used the powdered horn of animals and in this country years ago weaklings took tablets to make them more manly.'

The inspector laughed richly – 'more manly' – as a needle slid into Muller's arm and a tube was inserted in his rectum. At first Muller felt no more than discomfort, mainly from the constriction of the belt, but an increasing warmth from his genitals made it difficult to keep still. He had an irresistible desire to scratch his head, but the attendants held his arms firmly.

The warmth gave way to an ache, an ache that became an intense pain. It lasted two or three minutes. Muller held his breath. He held it until his lungs seemed to shudder violently and he writhed and gasped as the pain became intolerable. There were leads attached to the case and the doctor stood looking into the case at a dial. Once he looked at Muller and frowned.

The more rigidly Muller tried to hold himself the more he writhed. He was no stranger to pain. Once he had broken a leg; the previous winter he had fallen awkwardly and cracked two ribs. Painful; that had been painful; but not like this. Spasms shook him until his whole body was palpitating in tortured wavelets. His legs, at first rigid, now trembling, twisted sharply as Muller tried to kick out; the doctor turned the dial quickly and pressed a switch.

The pain ceased. As it did so electric shock-like stabs transfixed Muller's increasingly cataleptic being. From the region of his swollen genitals sensory eruptions inflamed him until his body shuddered in a final convulsive discharge.

The police girl, a shade paler, watched breathlessly, her teeth showing a little.

'Splendid,' breathed the inspector. 'Splendid!'

*

Night came. For some hours Muller had a vague sort of feeling that he was in bed, but nothing was certain. He was comfortable; infinitely relaxed; not asleep but with only the most unformed perception of consciousness.

Occasionally he stirred slightly. For years he had been a poor sleeper; his bed at home faced the window and he left the curtains partially undrawn. He couldn't sleep sometimes even with the aid of drugs and he didn't like total darkness. And for some reason or other he had never taken to reading in bed, so he would lie for hours facing the segment of sky, thinking of this and that. Always his mind centred on literary affairs, on the books he had written and hoped to write. The seriousness of his position had worried him increasingly in recent years, and that – the worry and anxiety – was a bad thing to go to bed with, it made a poor start to the night. But after an hour or so in bed it wasn't so bad; somehow or other he managed to attain calmness, everything fell into shape with a surprising but sustaining optimism, and dreams of a better future possessed him.

It was two hours or so usually before he slept, but some nights he fell to sleep quickly and awoke abruptly in the middle of the night. Those were bad nights; he had never fully recovered from the death of his parents, and when he awoke abruptly like that they flashed before him in an alarming way. They seemed to be in front of him right there in the room, and they (to Muller) seemed to gesture in a cautionary sort of way. They seemed to be warning him of something. Muller knew it was all nerves and imagination, with an underlying basis of fear, but he was always upset, and couldn't sleep afterwards. He took a nembutal capsule, and that soothed him, but it didn't always bring sleep.

His bed faced the window and he started off lying on his right side. The first hour in bed was usually an unknown quantity (he rarely felt the same two nights running) but the worst was usually over before he turned to his left side. After an hour on his left side he turned over again, and (usually) drifted towards sleep. He didn't time himself, of course, or look at the clock, but that's how it had started; for the first year or so of his insomnia it had been hell getting to sleep, he had looked at the clock again and again, turning repeatedly from one side to the other. Finally he had disciplined himself to lying for an hour on his right side before turning to his left, and an hour on his left side before turning to his right. It had become a habit. He rarely looked at his watch now, but a train (if one had been left) could have been timed by him.

Muller left the curtains undrawn at the extreme left and right of the window. It was a small room and the foot of his bed was close to the window. Whether he was on his right side or his left he could see a slab of sky or (on the darkest night) a drab rectangle not utterly obliterating, but he could see better on his right side than his left. This baffled Muller. The bed was – almost exactly – the same width as the window, and Muller made it carefully. Although not particularly neat he made his bed with an almost mathematical precision. And the curtains at each side of the window were undrawn for four inches; about four inches; that was enough. In theory, therefore, the patch of light at each side of the window should have been equally discernible, but it wasn't; the one on the right always seemed much the clearer.

It was one of those minor things that baffled Muller. There was nothing in the room – furniture – and nothing outside (trees or buildings) that shadowed the left side of the window, but there it was. Muller had mentioned the problem to McAllister, and McAllister had snorted.

'You and your insomnia!' he had scoffed. 'The great thing with insomnia is never to have it.'

'Never?'

'Certainly. Or very seldom.'

'It's not as easy as that.'

'Not as easy as that!' McAllister had cried gustily. 'Of course it is! It's not once in a blue moon I can't get to sleep and I soon cure *that*. Take three capsules and go out like a light. Snore well into the next morning and *that* gives the old sleep cycle a firm kick in the pants.'

'*Three* capsules?' Muller had asked.

'Certainly! You've taken them for years and I suppose you're afraid to take more than one, thinking you'll conk out or something. Don't worry!' McAllister had cried. 'It may never happen, and if it does I'll raise a stone in the Garden of Memory.

Here lies Muller
Wapsaw now's a little duller.'

*

Muller stirred as he lay in bed at Block Y. The borderline between sleep and awareness was a state long familiar to him and it was not a condition he liked. With most people it probably didn't matter, and to them it probably wasn't unpleasant: to be not asleep but not aware, or to be not awake but not sufficiently asleep to entirely exclude (now and then) the stirrings of perception. Muller disliked the condition because it was (to him) so susceptible to the strains and fears within him. He preferred to be fully awake or deeply asleep; when he was awake he could with some degree of logic attempt to grapple with his fears and problems, and when he was fully asleep all he knew usually was oblivion: it was rare for him to dream.

But in the lighter form of unconsciousness varying degrees of awareness would transport him from fantasy to fear – and reality – with terrifying abruptness. He would dream, and his dreams were complex and frightening – so real that when he emerged from them he would (with a conscious imagination but an incomplete realization of what he was doing) continue with his dream adventures. It wasn't easy sometimes to emerge from this state of fantasy; there were times when Muller wasn't sure whether he was awake and consciously imagining, or asleep and dreaming that he was dreaming.

But there was – more often than not – nothing frightening in that. On the difficult nights he rarely dreamed. He would lie then in a sleep so light that he would stir every half-hour or hour and gaze at the window for a few minutes before dozing again. And it was then, when he was on the edge of sleep, that something happened that terrified him. And he didn't know what it was. It was something (indefinable, unformed) deep in his mind that exploded unpredictably. It flashed through him as quickly as light, an intense fear that made him jump up in bed, his heart racing. Muller would take a sedative quickly, but it was usually some time before he calmed down, then he would lie staring at the window. It was so intense a fear that Muller tried to thrust it from him, tried (the next day) not to think of it, and it was a long time before he had mentioned it to McAllister.

'Indefinable?' said McAllister (who had taken a degree in psychology).

'Damned if I know.'

'It happens so quickly,' Muller had said. 'Within a second or so. There's a sort of gathering of unformed things. They seem to be merging into a definite shape – of a person or something. And then – wham.'

'It's simple enough, I suppose,' McAllister had said. 'Fear of your whole situation. You should have led a different life, my lad. Steadier, securer, more orthodox.'

'I couldn't have led a different life,' Muller had protested.

'I know – and that's the hell of it. But,' said McAllister, 'there's no need to be afraid. A psycho-analyst would straighten it out very quickly.'

'Would it be wise to go to one?'

'It would not,' McAllister had said gloomily.

There was the risk (after the whole background had been considered) that one might be classified as undesirable. That meant extinction.

*

Towards the middle of the night Muller stirred uneasily. There was a disturbance centre, an increasing agitation that disordered his sleep. It was the glare. At home he slept in the dark. There was the comforting misty dab from the partially uncurtained window, but that, after all, wasn't much. He slept in the dark. And now as he tossed fretfully in Arm T of Block Y he became increasingly aware of light. His room was not only (in effect) a glass box brilliantly illuminated from within: batteries of lights beat on it from without.

When Muller opened his eyes he lay still for several minutes. He felt calm; not as he felt usually when emerging from a dream. But Muller – who liked dim lights – knew he must be dreaming: it was a horrible sort of dream in which lights blinded him. Even with his eyes closed there was no relief. The glare got through; there was a reddish sort of haze. But he wanted to open his eyes, not close them, he wanted to see, he had to see, but he couldn't. When he opened his eyes the lights blinded him.

Muller began to breathe more rapidly. His right hand groped out for the bedside table. It couldn't find it. The hand was poised as Muller tried to suppress his alarm; carefully, in widening circles, the hand explored; it hung motionless again as Muller ('I must be dreaming; I must be') lay very still for a moment; then with a huge breath he bounded upright – and it all came back.

He sank down to the pillows, breathing heavily, a hand over his eyes. For one awful moment panic almost overwhelmed him, but the hand shielding his eyes touched his hair – hanging lankly – and jerked it back, and struck something. At once he felt better. Before they had come for him he had painted a tiny cardboard box the colour of his hair, crammed twelve capsules into it, and gummed it to his scalp. He had a good head of hair and the box was well-covered, but he knew he would be searched and examined. They would cut his hair probably and probe his body. He thought discovery of the box was almost certain, but it was still there.

It probably wouldn't have been there if his reception had been more orthodox, Muller conjectured. His mouth tightened. He couldn't believe that new arrivals were treated as he had been. It was possible, of course, but the doctor had seemed reluctant. No, it was the girl. The inspector would choose a girl like that – young and pretty – for a secretary, and she was new probably. Seen nothing like that before. Just the sort of show a fat sadist like that would delight in putting on: he would delight in horrifying her, fascinating her, and – finally – corrupting her.

Muller lay breathing heavily. The memory of it fired him again with shame and anger. 'Swine,' he muttered. 'Swine.' He must have fainted; but it was no ordinary faint. He had felt hazy but tranquil, as though emerging from a deep sleep; he thought he had been asleep, he had gazed up at what he thought was his bedroom ceiling at home, and there they were staring down at him. Unconsciousness must have followed awareness; the next thing he knew he was lying on an examination couch and the doctor was bending over him. As from a long way off he heard the inspector saying: 'Better give him a shot and we'll take him to his remedial extension. A fitting abode for one who has been remedially extended.'

Slowly – almost fearfully – Muller explored his body. It was warm, unusually warm, and his genitals were enlarged and swollen. As he snatched his hand away they began to ache savagely. Holding his breath Muller fought against the pain. As he writhed he reviled himself. He had waited for them to fetch him, waited like a child, and, in the box gummed in his scalp, there was escape, final and complete. He could have killed himself. And he could now. He could rip the box from his head and chew six of the capsules and it would soon be over. Oblivion.

'You're afraid,' Muller reviled himself. Afraid, afraid to die. There would be more degradation and torture ending, almost certainly, in death. And he was in pain now, and he could die now. And if suicide was abandonment of hope, had he not abandoned hope? 'Have I?' Muller tried to ask himself. Every man, the Superintendent had said, had the right to go fishing. There had been decency in the Superintendent, and in the constables, and in (for she was shocked and appalled) the police girl. But men like the inspector ruled the roost. What hope could there be, what hope, if people wouldn't fight?

The pain eased suddenly, and Muller sat up. The light drenched him in its brilliance, and Muller thrust out a hand and sank back to the pillows. Breathing heavily, he tried to think. He tried, he tried to think.

Up on the roof two guards paused in their walk.

'The new arrival seems restless,' said one, gazing down at Arm T.

The other stared. 'Old Veale had him in his office.'

'What did he do?'

'Who?'

'Veale.'

'I dunno. You know what he is.'

'Old bastard. Have you seen his new bit of stuff?'

The second guard grunted, and swung his arms. 'She could try walking out.'

'Think she'd get far?'

'They never try.'

Chapter 5

The next day they gave him a job. Two guards came and gave him a suit of black blouse and trousers and stood each side of him in the lift. It sank far below ground level and there was a maze then of passages with guards here and there. They passed heavy sliding steel doors and (to Muller's surprise) entered a machine shop. The machines were large and elaborate, each of a different type, but the machine-winders were dressed uniformly, and most of them were baldish, with drawn faces that looked sickly in the blue glare. None of them looked up, but before Muller could gather more definite impressions they had passed through the machine shop and were walking along a quiet passage. This led to a room where twenty or so men, white-coated, most of them, were bent over complex patterns, weird pinkish things about the size of a cistern. In a corner of the room was a small glass office occupied by a fattish grey-suited man, bespectacled and sombre. 'Muller, sir,' said one of the guards; and they saluted, and left.

The job seemed easy. He sat on a stool, his back touching the manager's (the office was too small), and he had a ledge on which to write, a narrow shelf not a foot wide. Facing him was a battery of card indexes and to his right was a recess. In the recess were sheets of paper, quarto-sized, and of almost every imaginable colour. Typed on the paper (sometimes one or two to a sheet, sometimes twenty or thirty) were numbers that Muller entered on the reference cards. What it was all about he didn't know. L(A)1/1745/8629 rcd. 2.7.93. rtd. 3.2.94. and A(GT) 1/297/7643 rcd. 24.4.94. were the first two references he recorded, and although the indexing of a seemingly inexhaustible supply of such references was hardly original literary work, he did at least feel better for having a pen in his hands.

But it did seem odd. The card index cabinet was of wood, and the drawers were heavy wooden things. Muller had been recording for some time before it occurred to him that the cabinet must be very old; it was not only made of wood but of genuine wood, wood from a tree; even forty or fifty years ago such things were – surely – made of pressed steel. 'Oh well,' he thought; 'all sorts of odds and ends tucked away in cellars survived the nuclear war.'

The drawers to the far left of him – A to K – were four feet or so away and not easy to reach from the stool. After Muller had hopped on and off the stool a few times he resolved to do the job standing; it would be in every way more comfortable; the drawers were not only heavy and difficult to reach, the stool was low and the ledge rather high. But, after Muller had been standing for a few minutes, the manager said coldly, 'You're to do the job sitting down. That's what the stool's there for. It's to sit on.'

Muller burned and said nothing. After an hour his neck began to ache and the powerful light three feet above his head stifled him. The paper (bright blue, pale pink, dull red, glaring green) on which the reference numbers were typed strained his eyes and his head started to throb. Three or four times white-coated men came in and (without speaking to him) hunted through the drawers and glanced at a card. This convinced Muller that his job was a bona-fide one; presumably the men were checking the date on which a pattern had been returned or received; but when the manager went out for a few minutes he looked at the stool: the legs had been shortened recently, probably that morning. Muller's fingerprints had been taken; he had been photographed, weighed and measured; and he wondered if everything (the stool, ledge, cabinet) had been installed or altered after his measurements were known.

The cards certainly were genuine. Some of them were old and faded and some of the dates went back years. But they were uncommonly large; about twice the usual size, and awkward to handle on the narrow ledge. It wasn't too bad when there were few entries on the cards; Muller sat back on the stool, so that the bottom part of the card projected over the ledge. But when there was little space on the cards – most of them needed replacing, but something told him not to ask for new cards – Muller turned them sideways, and scrawled in the entry as best he could. When he did this he wriggled round on the stool, and once – out of the corner of his eye – saw the manager opening a small attaché case. The manager's desk was large and low and the case was no more than two or three feet from Muller. There was nothing in the case except a piece of cake, a large piece about 2 lb. in weight. The manager was studying a blueprint and he had opened the case without taking his eyes from the drawing. Still gazing at the drawing he broke off a huge lump of cake and stuffed it into his mouth. Muller stared as though hypnotized. Calmly, casually and efficiently the manager's jaws champed until his mouth was empty. For a moment he paused, then – still staring at the drawing – he made a sudden gurgling noise, and his hand groped for the case and broke off another huge lump of cake.

After a wretched night Muller had been unable to face the grey watery porridge that (with a warning shriek from the whistle) had appeared for breakfast. He wasn't just hungry, his whole body felt empty in a sick, horribly aching sort of way. He stared at the cake and saliva poured into his mouth. He licked his lips and turned back to the cabinet.

*

Towards the end of the second day every item on the sheets of paper had been recorded. Muller hesitated for quite a time, then he turned to the manager, and said,

'Excuse me. I've cleared up the arrears of work. Can I have something to do?'

The manager (who hadn't spoken since reprimanding him) stared uncomprehendingly, and said: 'What?'

Muller waved towards the pile of paper, and repeated his request.

The manager was silent for some time, then he said quietly: 'Well. You've done a good job. Better fetch some more papers.'

Muller blinked. '*Fetch* some?'

'Go along the passage into the machine shop,' said the manager. 'Go to the top end of the shop. You'll see a little man – Mr Edkins – at a desk. Ask him.'

Muller's heart beat wildly. To be allowed to walk about unescorted! 'Thanks,' he said. 'And the record cards. Do you think I might have a fresh supply?'

The manager nodded. 'I'll get some. And Muller – don't do anything silly. A press of a button – less than a second – and fifty doors between here and the lifts will close.'

Muller walked along the passage. The faint nagging hum that for the best part of two days had lived in his throbbing head swelled to a roar as he entered the machine shop. Dazed, he stood for a moment, then turned to the right, between a row of machines. The floor was littered with metal objects, some small, some large, and overhead hoists dangled massive sections close to his head. The machines were large, twenty feet long some of them, with projectories and moving parts that Muller scurried past apprehensively. Twice he nearly impaled himself as he leapt from the path of automatic trucks, then a guard took his elbow and asked what he wanted. 'Edkins!' bawled Muller. 'Edkins! Mr Edkins!'

The top part of the shop – two hundred yards away – was much quieter. There was no machinery and the atmosphere was measured. Here and there on the floor were newly manufactured items and one weird object – a huge thing, some form of weapon, thought Muller – was being stared at critically by a group of substantial-looking men.

In the top right corner was a small bespectacled man standing at a small desk.

'I-I'm from the manager's office,' stammered Muller. 'He says can I have some more papers. The record sheet things – the papers with the reference numbers.'

Mr Edkins – elderly and frog-faced – stared disapprovingly.

'Record sheet things. And what might your name be?'

'Muller.'

'You don't make yourself very clear, Mr Muller. What is your occupation normally?'

'A sort of writer.'

'A *sort* of writer!' Mr Edkins said severely. 'Full of strange ideas about everything under the sun, I suppose?'

'Well,' Muller hesitated. 'I used to be.'

'Used to be!' echoed the outraged Mr Edkins. 'Used to be! Without any idea of how to make anything under the sun.'

'Not when I was young,' Muller admitted.

'And now you find yourself here. And can you wonder at it? It's time,' Mr Edkins said severely, 'time you were converted.'

'Converted?'

'Certainly. Converted to the scientific way of life. To the world that makes things.'

'Well,' Muller began. 'It makes things but –'

'But!' snapped Mr Edkins. 'But! There you go, you see. *But*.' He shook his head. 'You're a bad case. You'll have to be drained.'

'Drained?'

'Certainly. Drained. You know what draining is?'

Muller shook his head, and Mr Edkins pursed his twisted lips.

'It reminds me of people who've had a big operation. You know the people I mean. They need a major operation but they look – some of them – well and healthy with a good colour and plenty of go.'

'True.'

'Ah! But see them immediately after the operation and what do they look like? Aha!' Mr Edkins said with relish, 'what do they look like after the knife's been at work? What do they look like *then*? Stopped their gallops, hasn't it?'

'Yes,' said Muller, 'but –'

'There you go again,' snapped Mr Edkins. '"Yes, but" instead of "but, yes". Instead of saying – or thinking – it's kind of the authorities not to kill me but to attempt a major reconversion job you persist in your wilful illogicality.'

'Reconversion job?' blinked Muller.

'Certainly! Don't you think you need one?'

'Well,' Muller said wearily. 'I don't know.' He touched his head. 'I need something. But . . .' the little man's garrulity after two days of silence and misery was too much . . . 'the sadism. The torture . . .'

'Torture?' Mr Edkins said sharply. He looked round and his manner changed. 'Muller,' he said softly, his eyes darting about furtively, 'give thanks that you're classified as a brain worker. A professional man. Have you seen the poor devils who operate the machines?'

Muller stared.

'It's a skilled job – you wouldn't learn it in ten years – a skilled job and a demanding job. But they're classified as manual workers and they're no more than slaves. Torture,' hissed the little man, 'has to *end*. They'll tire of you one way or another in a week or so. But those men are housed in guarded barracks and worked until –'

He broke off; one of the beefy white-coated men was drifting towards them.

'But skilled men are valuable,' frowned Muller. 'What have they done?'

'Here,' Mr Edkins said sharply, producing two typed sheets. 'These are all I have at the moment. I may have more later.'

On the way back to the office the guard appeared. 'I'll

show you the best route. It's dangerous getting too near to some of these machines.'

The path between the machines began narrowly: it was about six feet wide until it turned a corner to a wide central aisle. As they turned the corner McAllister passed them. He was dressed in the black blouse and trousers and he was haggard and balding, but there was no doubt of it: it was McAllister.

'What's the matter?' the guard bawled.

Muller shook his head and moved on. 'Nothing. Felt a bit faint.'

'It's the machines,' the guard shouted. 'Dig your fingernails into each other an' it'll pass off.'

Back in the office Muller sat down shakily. His heart was still beating feverishly.

'Machines,' he said.

The manager stared. 'Machines?'

'Scared me a bit.'

The manager laughed – not without pride. 'Don't like my machines, eh?'

Muller forced himself to laugh.

'Amazing things. Marvellous. But a little fearsome.'

The manager laughed again and reached for his case.

*

At 6 p.m. the pattern-makers and mock-up men went home. So did the manager. So did Muller. At 5.57 p.m. a guard came for him and escorted him through the machine shop (still working) and along the passages to the lift. The guard pressed the button for 29T and they walked along the narrow passage that led directly to the door of Arm T. It was like a walk to an execution chamber.

In accordance with the Rules for Detainees Muller washed, changed into the white transparent suit and sat down in the egg-shaped transparent chair. He had to remain like that until the whistle screeched at 7 p.m. for supper. His back and arms ached, his neck burned fiercely and his head throbbed sickeningly, but Muller was conscious only of two things: McAllister and thirst.

He had jotted down the reference numbers as quickly as possible, and twice made the journey for more record sheets. Each time he had been disappointed. His heart had raced excitedly and his tongue seemed glued to the roof of his mouth, but Mr Edkins was busy, and there was no sign of McAllister. Mr Edkins had waved his hand brusquely (the first time there had been *one* record sheet on his desk; the second time three) and Muller had felt quite angry. His initial surprise at seeing McAllister had turned to excitement and confusion. He couldn't understand why McAllister was here, and what he was doing; but for his dress and ravaged face Muller would have found it hard to believe he was a prisoner. But he was, he was; he was employed in or near the machine shop; and he couldn't see him.

There was no cup or glass in the room, no vessel that could be used for drinking. Muller hesitated, then jumped up and went to the wash bowl and drank again and again from his cupped hands. He felt better; but before he was back in the chair a voice – as from nowhere – demanded to know what he was doing.

'Drinking water,' said Muller.

'Water, eh?' sneered the voice.

'I'm sorry,' said Muller. 'I've felt unwell all afternoon.'

'You'll feel worse if you don't stick to the rules,' said the voice.

Muller writhed. You bastard, he said to himself; you bastard. For the first time in his life he felt an urge to kill; the tension of the afternoon that had constricted his chest gripped his body as though the whole of it was a burning sinew. His fist clenched as he took a shuddering breath. 'You bastard,' he said. 'You bastard.' In the centuries before progress came men had killed and tortured in the name of this cause and that: some men still did so: for sport, and for a living.

When supper came he threw it – soup and a hunk of bread – down him, then stared fixedly before him until the apparatus (bowl on a rod with spoon attached) sank again into the floor. It was a clinical dentist's surgery sort of contraption, repulsive, but preferable to the arrangements for dinner. That was served at 1 p.m. A guard took him through the machine shop and along a passage lined with cell doors and locked him in Cell 97. There was an aperture with a stool below and a lavatory basin. The cell for that matter was about the size of the smallest lavatory, and the stool (fixed to the floor) by some ingenious arrangement seemed to be part of the basin. It was within an inch or so of it; sitting on it one was impeded by the basin; sitting on the basin one was impeded by the seat of the stool. The basin reeked (sanitation in the depths of Block Y must be something of a problem) and the aperture through which dinner appeared – stew in a metal bowl fixed to a sliding panel some ten inches square – was almost directly over the basin.

'Bastards,' said Muller.

Bathed in the intense brilliance of the lights – which would ruin his eyes in a few weeks – he stared straight before him and wondered if McAllister (in accordance with the Rules) was sitting similarly in his own remedial extension. Muller shook and almost exploded into laughter. How he would (in different circumstances) have loved hearing McAllister on the whole subject. McAllister was an extremely vigorous and mobile character, and to think of him as he was now was almost too much.

'Something the matter?' demanded the voice.

'Indigestion,' said Muller. 'I'm sorry.'

'Serves you right,' said the voice. 'Bolted your supper in less than two minutes, you greedy pig.'

Five minutes was allowed for supper and (there was the lavatory basin to contemplate) sixty minutes for the midday meal. The extremely close confinement of the cells was unpleasant, and Muller could imagine it unnerving some people, but one was at least alone, and the vile stink didn't disturb Muller unduly: his sense of smell was deficient. McAllister, on the other hand, was no lover of solitude and – although a stronger character than Muller – was more inclined to be upset by trifles. And the little things apart he almost certainly hadn't escaped Inspector Veale's experiments.

Why was he here? Muller's face saddened. Their friendship was perhaps surprising: McAllister for all his fiery vehemence was fundamentally orthodox, even a little staid and prim. Basically he was a solid schoolmaster type. His youth was unblemished and he had left university with a bland assurance, but he had – oddly – found it difficult to settle. McAllister put it down to an itch for travel that he couldn't satisfy now that travelling was virtually impossible. But he had journeyed from one job to another, and they had met when McAllister was at the crossroads: thwarted in love and at loggerheads with his chief at the Civic Palace Planning Office.

McAllister – very much in love – was violently unhappy, and every night for a month he poured out an astonishing stream of nonsense. Muller listened patiently, then with an increasing boredom and irritation that he found difficult to conceal, but McAllister was much better, and approached one of his old lecturers, who wangled him a job as a teacher. McAllister lasted one term at his first school – a Junior Preselection Mixed – and two terms at his second, then he found a school that he liked and settled down so well that his head – after two years – called him a 'credit to his chosen profession'. Muller – seeing less of his old friend – smiled: McAllister's increasing security was becoming just a little too apparent. Off-duty he could, with a few drinks in him, be as incendiary as ever, but it was obvious that his travelling days were over. Then out of the blue had come a message from the Office of Education. McAllister was (for no apparent reason) to be transferred to 'a school elsewhere'. McAllister had stormed off angrily to the Office of Education and was seen no more.

Muller closed his eyes tightly for a moment, then stared up and down, and to his left and right. He could see nothing. The lights although immensely powerful were so cunningly designed and positioned that one prisoner couldn't see another. People were there, only a few yards away, but all Muller could see was a sort of milky phosphorescence hung in the glare of what seemed an impossibly fierce sun. Muller's eyes throbbed; he closed them again; in a blinding concentration of light he was blind.

Today was Thursday or Friday – he wasn't sure which – and on Saturday there was his engagement with Kitty One-Eye. He hadn't – yet – worried much about it; he had been in so much misery that the thought of more degradation was impossible to grasp. To go on like this was out of the question, but what was the alternative? They were unlikely to release him and escape seemed impossible. That left the simple choice of death, and to die would be easy. It would also be subservient, utterly so. Muller's mouth tightened. His face burned as anger rose in him. Opening his eyes he glared into the pitiless torture of the lights.

*

Next morning at 10 a.m. the Manager (not a man who would have corn flakes for breakfast) left the office quickly, and Muller, who was out of reference sheets, got up and walked into the machine shop. He walked to the lower end of the shop – towards the doors and passages that led to the lifts – then retraced his steps with the air of a man who was confused and lost. No one questioned him or even looked at him, but he was glad when he reached the little man's desk.

'Found it?' Mr Edkins asked laconically.

Muller started.

'You're holding your breath and your eyes are too furtive,' said Mr Edkins. 'You must be more careful.'

Muller tried to say something and Mr Edkins tapped his pencil.

'I know your friend. At least I knew his parents. So did my wife. Knew them well. It was a shock when I saw Neil here.'

'He's *done* nothing,' Muller said violently. 'He's *done* nothing. He –'

Mr Edkins stopped him. 'He lost his temper. Slapped a little beast whose father – he's on the Committee – got straight on to the Director of Education. They went over Neil's dossier and found him unsatisfactory. Inflammatory talk, undesirable associates.'

'Of all the nonsense!' Muller said angrily. 'McAllister was doing well and –'

'I know,' Mr Edkins cut in sharply. 'I know. Apart from one or two blemishes they thought him all right professionally, so they gave him another chance.'

'He went to the office –'

'Went to the office and blew his top when they told him he was being transferred to Banff.'

'Banff?'

'A remote place in Scotland. Neil in any case would have been dismissed – his tongue got the better of him – but one of Jallen's men heard him so he was brought here.'

'Jallen,' said Muller. 'Can they hear us?'

'No,' Mr Edkins snapped irritably. 'Hidden cameras and mikes and whatnot are old-fashioned. No: the Secretary of Personnel saw Neil and told him he was being transferred to Banff. Neil went mad. Stormed off to the Director's office. They'd been tipped off, of course, but Neil wouldn't take no for an answer. Cussed the Director's secretary and tried to force his way past her. And *that*,' Mr Edkins said sadly, 'was too bad, because Jallen's man had sort of dropped in to see her: she's his girl friend.'

'Poor McAllister.' Muller clenched his fists.

The little man gazed up at him. 'He saw you yesterday. He wants to meet you. But it won't do you much good if you're seen talking together.'

'It surprises me,' said Muller. 'Being allowed to move about like this.'

The little man smiled grimly. 'Just playing with you.

Your – what shall we call it? Passivity. Acceptance. But they'll think of something.'

'They have,' said Muller. 'I have an engagement with a Kitty One-Eye for Saturday.'

'Sexual business? It's their main hobby. Now listen,' said Mr Edkins, 'I'm mad trying to help you. I'm taking my life in my hands. And there's not much I can do. I don't think you'll get out of the main block and if you do where can you go? You'll be captured and killed.'

'If we stay?' asked Muller. 'What then?'

'After they've finished with you you may be alive and sane. You may be but I doubt it.'

'Is that why you want to help us?'

'No. No,' said Mr Edkins, pouching his froggy little face, 'I don't think so. I've seen hundreds of detainees and it hasn't bothered me. I just feel a bit differently now because – well – I don't know; let's say it's because I knew Neil's people.'

Muller stared at the little man. In the most elaborate and cleverly conceived structures there were sometimes elementary faults. In Block Y there were hundreds of guards and policemen linked to an inhuman and complex organization. And here was Mr Edkins. Could he be trusted? His mere existence – and availability – seemed ludicrous.

'It's odd,' he said. 'For years I've met only two or three people with minds of their own. But in these last two or three days several people I've met have seemed – well – different.'

'That,' said Mr Edkins, 'is because you've met people on the inside. On the inside looking out if you like. The people outside are outside and afraid to look in. If you see what I mean.'

'I do,' said Muller. He hesitated. 'Do you live here in Block Y, Mr Edkins?'

The little man stared. 'No,' he said slowly. 'No. Used to but it's such a vile place. Got on my wife's nerves.' He looked around him. 'Now listen. We hadn't better talk too long. Now' – and his eyes swivelled warningly – 'take these sheets and come back later. This afternoon say. But I won't be able to do anything before Monday. Stick it till then.'

'Monday,' said Muller.

'Radiation,' hissed Mr Edkins. 'Start a panic.' He prodded the reference sheets as if explaining something. 'Now don't turn your head – no! – keep your head still but look to your left. See that door over there? Guard near it. It's your only chance. That door,' croaked Mr Edkins, 'is the entrance to a lift that's reserved for the bosses. Used two or three times a day. Sometimes not that. The guard gets bored and walks around a bit to stretch his legs. Not far. Ten yards this way, ten yards that. But you might just slip past without him noticing.'

Muller watched tensely. The door was in the opposite corner of the shop, about fifty yards away. The guard lounging near by looked quite elderly. As Muller watched he yawned, a slow, heavy yawn. Then he strolled a few yards to a small crate, yawned again, and sat down, facing the door.

'The lift goes straight to the executive floor. It's quiet up there but there are warning lights and guards and what-not. What you could *do* if you get up there I don't know. But,' Mr Edkins said bleakly, 'it's your only chance.'

His mind racing, Muller walked back through the machine shop. It seemed pointless to put off the attempt until Monday. And a panic might make the escape more difficult. He had no idea what Edkins had in mind but an emergency wouldn't help. There might be confusion initially, but there would be (very quickly in Block Y surely) additional security measures. Surprise was the best element. If, thought Muller, *if* I could see McAllister I'd make a break now.

Because of his excitement he walked quickly, and entered the office quite briskly. He was returning to misery, but there was *hope* now: in a few hours' time he would see Edkins (and, perhaps, McAllister) again, and attempt a break. To hell with waiting for Monday, and, for that matter, Saturday night.

In the office he stopped dead. A guard was awaiting him. The guard – huge and stolid – stifled a yawn and said: 'Inspector Veale wants to see you.'

Muller must have paled, for the guard took the reference sheets off him and said reassuringly: 'Nothing to worry about. He just wants a chat.'

Muller glanced at the manager – who was carefully studying a blueprint – and followed the guard. His legs felt the least bit quivery and his chest felt painfully constricted again. He had thought Edkins too good to be true, but even if he was not what doubt could there be – in spite of the guard's reassurance – that their plans had been discovered? But the fat inspector – who was minus his pretty secretary – smiled wanly and said: 'Muller. Ah. Sit down.'

The guard saluted and left and Muller sat down tensely.

'Well,' said the inspector – his eyes were glazed and his breathing noisy again. 'Well. They tell me you have settled down remarkably well and taken most of the er – little inconveniences in your stride.'

Muller said nothing, and the inspector took a breath and – in mid-air as it were – enlarged the ensuing exhalation to a prodigious yawn.

'Tired. Annual dinner last night.' He yawned again and blew his nose. 'Well, Muller. I congratulate you. Most detainees go a bit potty after two nights and we put them down if the experimental people don't want them. Weaklings.' He rubbed his eyes with his huge hand, then – taking a lilac-coloured handkerchief from a drawer – wiped his face carefully. 'Courage, as I never point out – it's not fashionable – doesn't always go with a good physique. Often the opposite.'

'Always thought I was a bit of a coward,' Muller said jerkily.

'I don't know. Perhaps you have something else. But,' the inspector sighed, 'I've been looking at some of your early writing, and some of your more recent stuff. And I've reached an astonishing conclusion.'

'Oh,' said Muller. 'Why?' He bent towards the inspector, who eased himself farther from his desk, and closed his eyes. For fully two or three minutes he seemed to be trying to regulate his breathing, then he opened his eyes and said, 'Odd.'

'Odd?' asked Muller, but the inspector closed his eyes again, breathing heavily but more evenly until he seemed to be asleep. Tensely Muller watched him; he knew he hadn't been sent for just for a chat.

After about thirty seconds – it seemed much longer – the pretty police girl looked in. She stood at the door uncertainly and averted her eyes when Muller glanced at her. As the door closed Muller's legs twitched: he almost followed her. In the vicinity were dozens of policemen but they wouldn't expect a prisoner to escape from the chief-inspector's office. 'But,' thought Muller, 'if I dodge them how far can I get? Where can I go? What can I do?' The problems would be similar when he attempted to escape with McAllister, but there would – Muller hoped – be a time-lag before their absence was noticed, and arrangements of some sort by old Edkins (a supply of food perhaps) that would give them a better chance.

The inspector took a last mighty breath through his nose, opened his eyes, and said: 'You're a romantic.'

Muller blinked. 'A romantic?'

The inspector adjusted his bulk carefully, and sighed. 'You have – by the Committee – acquired a reputation of a sort of cold intellectual. A reactionary with unpopular ideas and theories. An enemy of society. But I'm convinced that you're no more than a sentimentalist. A romantic. If,' sighed the inspector, 'if only you'd had two or three nice little girls when you were young, and married another nice little girl you wouldn't be where you are now.'

Muller stared in some surprise and managed a laugh.

'Of course,' said the inspector, 'it's all a sort of throwback. Emotion has gone out. Personally – strangely you may think for a fat puff-ball of a man and a police officer to boot – personally I'm emotional. I feel strongly. I understand emotion. I am for that matter a practitioner in emotion.'

Muller flushed. 'Emotion?'

'All right. Perversion. But as I was saying although I regard you as a harmless romantic the Committee think otherwise. And years ago the people who felt strongly were the people who agitated and aroused feelings in others. That is no longer possible. People can't congregate. Not without being seen.'

Muller waited. On his way to the inspector's office he had expected the obvious. It hardly seemed credible that his talks with Edkins hadn't been recorded or observed, and his 'undesirable association' with McAllister was all too well known to them. But he had, of course, since his detention in Block Y – had only a brief glimpse of McAllister. He hadn't spoken to him.

'I have,' breathed the inspector, 'looked at copies of ancient journals. Conspiracy in the shadows, cartoons of bearded men in cloaks carrying home-made bombs. Marvellous!' He inhaled warmly. 'Fragments of clues that had to be pieced together by men using fingerprint powder and magnifying glasses.'

He laughed and his face flushed alarmingly as his belly shook.

'My favourite reading is from our old records. Reports – seventy years old some of them – of investigations into criminal cases. Many of them are oddly amusing. "I proceeded to the scene of the crime and viewed the body. Rigor mortis had set in."' The inspector shook again and wiped his eyes. 'I speak personally, of course, but it's too easy today ... The box, for instance, the little box glued to your head was spotted within a short time of your arrival here. The glue must be strong and' – the glassy eyes were almost warm for a moment – 'I admire you, my dear Muller, for choosing to live. The betting is at evens.'

'We could, of course,' the inspector breathed heavily, 'remove the box, and we don't want our arrangements for tomorrow night disrupted. But it's an unwritten law here that anyone wishing to die should be allowed to do so. And – it's nicely balanced, isn't it? – Kitty *may* not be able to appear.'

Muller tried to keep calm. 'She . . . hasn't another engagement?'

'May have,' said the inspector. 'With the devil. Poor old Kit's very poorly. But the doctors are working on her and if they fail they won't be popular with *me*.'

'With you. But *you* won't be unpopular if *I* commit suicide?'

The inspector took a breath and puffed out his cheeks.

'Well, your life history and our investigations point to the fact – coupled with my analysis of course – that you're not a suicidal type. But I'm concerned about you. I am,' said the inspector, 'concerned about you. By 8 p.m. tomorrow you'll be in a state. Awful state. And so I'm going to give you a marvellous drug that will put you to sleep until 7 p.m. tomorrow. No nasty side-effects or reactions. You'll awake feeling calm and well. Fit and strong and ready for battle. Now I may,' puffed the inspector, 'be wrong, but I am saving you a tremendous amount of anxiety and tension – together with a very bad night probably – so I do think in all the circumstances that I'm doing you a real service. Don't you agree?'

Muller looked at the fat puff-ball. He hated him and feared him, but at this moment he – oddly enough – felt little emotion. 'In the circumstances I suppose so. Particularly with the betting at evens.'

The inspector's flesh shook as he laughed. 'I must,' Muller told himself, 'keep calm. Somehow I must get through to Monday.' His mind was convulsive, but Monday was a peg with which he tried to hold it together.

'And it is,' he said, his voice curiously flat, 'all so romantic.'

The inspector raised a fat white hand. 'But I meant what

I said. It does intrigue me. It's a thing personally – if I were dictator – that I would reward. If, of course, there were no social complications. How anyone,' said the inspector, 'can be a romantic in this scientific age baffles me.'

'I can be a realist,' said Muller.

'You think you can,' snapped the inspector. 'You think you can.' For a few seconds his cheeks showed a touch of red, then he relaxed, and laughed. 'No. It was people like you – a century ago – who agitated for improvements. They wanted better working conditons, plenty of leisure and so on. An ideal society. Seventy-odd years ago – in the nineteen-twenties shall we say – progressive people pictured perfection in terms of what? Of what, Muller?' he demanded.

Muller laughed harshly. 'Justice, I suppose. Not all of them saw perfection. But you seem to be the historian. Tell me.'

The inspector chuckled. He seemed to be genuinely gratified. 'You run true to type Muller. Can't face the facts. And the truth,' he wheezed, 'is that clever people – idealists, romantics – pictured the millennium as a sort of celestial city created by politics and science.' And the inspector's belly shook as he laughed again.

'What a combination!' His face reddened and he wiped his eyes, breathing painfully.

'Odds and ends – war, want, disease and so on – had been done away with, and there they were in their heaven on earth.'

He shook silently in what might have been a bronchial paroxysm.

'You have the makings of a comedian,' said Muller.

The inspector gasped and blew his nose. 'A what?'

'Comedian.'

'You think so?' The inspector struggled with his breathing. 'I'm gratified. There isn't much comedy about and it's one of the few things we have left, isn't it, Muller?'

He inhaled deeply. 'And it's a point. What visions of

the future include comedy? Understandably. But those people of the past lived in a squat little world, so one could expect their aspirations to soar. Soar they did.'

Muller tried to laugh but all he produced was a cough.

'Their vision of the future took the form of a city – a city of shining white towers. Perfection' – the inspector chuckled – 'can't be brighter than white, can it, Muller?'

Muller said nothing and the inspector laughed. 'So the natives – "to hell we sink, to heaven we soar," if you recall the old ditty, Muller – the natives were as handsome as gods and dressed like little girls in virginal shifts. Minor oddities like work had been done away with, but everybody was educated to professional standards, so they – in between whizzing up and down the white towers – sat around writing great poetry and great music and whatnot.'

'Don't be absurd,' Muller almost groaned.

'It is absurd, isn't it?' the inspector chuckled.

'But at least attractive. Idealistic in a simple way.'

'Exactly. So beautifully childish.'

'There's nothing *wrong* with it,' Muller almost snarled. 'It's a *clean* sort of image if nothing else. It's not *evil*.'

'The evil things, Muller,' the inspector smiled, 'always come. But there is something wrong there. Life for most people – in 1890 or 1990 – means work. Life is the ordinary man going home from work. Washing, eating, sitting on the lavatory seat; worrying, dreaming, making love and so on.'

'I'm not sure that I follow you,' said Muller. 'And I thought you didn't care about the ordinary man.'

'I don't,' the inspector replied. 'And neither do you, you idiot.'

Muller stared in some surprise. '*I* don't?'

The inspector frowned. 'Muller,' he said, taking a breath and exhaling sharply. 'Muller,' he said, 'when you were young – in your teens – you felt deeply about things. Books, music, poetry and so on. In short, art. That's what you cared about. Do you deny it?'

'I can't deny it,' Muller admitted gravely.

'Of course not. Now the position,' said the inspector, 'is this. A hundred years ago most people knew little about art and cared less. Fifty years ago people were beginning to care quite a lot. Am I right?'

Muller didn't answer and the inspector repeated his question. 'I suppose so,' said Muller. 'You seem to know.'

The inspector chuckled. 'Most people know a great deal about very little. Because I'm fond of reading – one of the few readers left, eh, Muller? – I know a bit about everything.' He took two or three breaths, and wagged a finger. 'But knowledge is one thing and art another. It's desirable but not essential. Most people can live without it. Think of religion. For centuries there was a belief in God, then untold millions of people were killed in the nuclear war, and bang went paradise. The survivors could have cried out for salvation, but they didn't. They just couldn't believe any more. Belief was a sort of idiocy.'

Muller winced. 'You're no fool. But there are all sorts of answers to that.'

The inspector laughed softly. 'The survivors found none – and I doubt if they sought any. There was one question: survival. The survivors concentrated on survival, and out went the trimmings. Out went most of the items that made a full life, as it was called.'

Muller's fist opened. 'Items?'

The inspector took a noisy breath. 'Art, Muller, is a sort of individuality. It does all sorts of interesting things, but it's not essential to ordinary workaday life.'

'Not essential?' said Muller. 'Come now!'

'Not,' said the inspector, 'to the masses. The more subtle forms could be corruptive, and other forms – such as television, which we banned – are like your friend McAllister. Chancy. A bit of a problem. Difficult to align with the times. But' – he smiled – 'the plain fact is that most people, as I have said, lost interest in art. And that's where you went wrong.'

Muller's temples were throbbing and he had gone pale. The fat devil was playing with him. McAllister at last had crept into it and Edkins would certainly emerge when the inspector felt like it.

Muller licked his lips. 'Went wrong? What do you mean?'

'I mean – try slow, deep breaths, it helps, Muller – I mean that people didn't share your interests. This set up a sort of disturbance centre, but your scorn was directed not at the people – and you hated them, even if you didn't realize it – but at the authorities.'

'What nonsense!' Muller burst out angrily. 'Far from hating those who didn't share my interests, I refused quite a few invitations years ago to talk and lecture to people because I was stupidly, idiotically nervous and shy. Does that go with hate?'

'Quite possibly,' the inspector replied suavely. 'And it's scarcely a defence.'

'I don't need a defence!' cried Muller. The blood pounding in his head, he jumped up. 'I don't *need* a defence,' he cried. 'For years I was self-sufficient. I knew a few people who shared my interests and I was indifferent about the rest. I didn't feel or think or care about them. Not in that sense anyway.'

The inspector chuckled. 'Not in that sense!' He waved a hand languidly. 'The truth – do sit down, Muller, before I knock you down – the truth is that you despised them. For years you despised them and your contempt grew to hatred. And,' said the inspector, 'I don't blame you for that. There's something wrong with a man who doesn't despise the masses. But you thought the answer to it all was to make every man the same as you. That wasn't possible or desirable; and it wasn't sensible.'

Muller – sitting down – laughed harshly. 'Not sensible!'

'Certainly not.' The inspector sighed gently. 'The ordinary man's life is his work. Always was and always will be. You should have separated the wheat from the chaff and gone to the people who would have supported you.'

Muller stared. 'Supported me? *Supported* me?'

The inspector took a long slow breath and exhaled

gently. 'Leisure,' he said, 'has never been the problem we expected. Most people are quite happy doing nothing when their day's work is over. Our Halls of Pleasure and so on have helped a lot, but when I say "doing nothing" I mean nothing of significance is needed to keep them going.' His thick grey eyebrows lifted. 'The *masses*. But with other people the problem is not so easy. And what do we find?'

'I don't know,' said Muller. 'What do we find?'

The inspector's eyes frosted for a moment. Then he smiled. 'Art in the main is frowned upon because of the images it can project. The whole thing passes logic. If, for instance, people see landscapes or sea pictures or listen to old music such as the *Pastoral* Symphony, they shouldn't be nostalgic or unhappy, because most of them have no experience of what they're seeing or hearing. But,' said the inspector, 'it doesn't work out like that.'

Muller laughed. 'It doesn't. But I thought things like the *Pastoral* were banned?'

The inspector puffed out his cheeks. 'Recordings exist. As a matter of fact we've experimented with groups of young people. For three days fed them such stuff. Shown them old films with country settings and so on. Concentrated course.'

'Interesting,' said Muller. The inspector was staring hard at him. He managed to keep his own eyes steady for a moment. 'What were the results?'

Slowly the inspector smiled. 'Muller, you're as emotional as a babe, but most of the time you manage to look like a stick of old seaweed. I like that.' And to Muller's surprise he jumped up and said petulantly: 'Results? Satisfactory with most of them. Interested and amused at first, then irritated and bored. No lasting impression.'

Muller watched him. 'And the rest of them? Those who weren't satisfactory?'

The inspector stared menacingly, then smiled and sat down. 'Interesting. A few needed treatment and one or two didn't respond. So you see' – he moved restlessly –

'that a sort of romantic movement in 1999 is undesirable. It's unrealistic. Chancy with the young. On the other hand' – he shrugged – 'I know one or two people who paint. That's rare enough nowadays – from where, for instance, do they get their materials? – and I certainly know people who like music. The real stuff. Take it in turns to entertain. Dinner with two hours or so of music afterwards.' The inspector smiled absently. 'I even know a woman who likes poetry. Nice woman too.'

Muller laughed. 'Nice! And the others. What sort of people are they?'

The inspector blew an impatient breath. 'Important obviously. Don't misunderstand me, Muller. Of the people who matter no more than a handful have such tastes. And they don't advertise them. The artistic instinct,' the inspector said carefully, 'isn't easy to repress, but I – speaking personally, of course – see no great harm in it if it's a secondary choice.'

Muller felt some surprise. '*Secondary* choice? What do you mean . . . as a sort of hobby?'

'Sort of,' agreed the inspector. 'A thing of maturity preferably. And preferably –'

'Don't tell me!' Muller exploded. 'For God's sake don't tell me! Preferably for sycophants. Occupationally sound. Morally acceptable. Politically impeccable.'

He was trembling slightly and the blood was throbbing again in his head. His temples ached and his eyes were so heavy with fatigue that his anger soon died.

The inspector sighed gently. 'I know, Muller. I know. My woolly arguments lead nowhere do they? Only to entanglements. But it's true what I say. The people I've mentioned aren't sycophants. They're orthodox certainly. Good citizens. But they do have this taste for art, and I've heard them mention your work. I'm sure they'd have done something for you – found you a sinecure, a soft little job or something, if –'

'If,' Muller interjected. '*If*,' he said wearily. 'If I'd been a different being. If I'd cut the ideas out.' He gestured, half in anguish, half in despair. 'Ten or fifteen years too late you tell me I've been a fool. Between bouts of torture you argue that I'm a stupid romantic and shouldn't be here at all. But . . . I'm here. I'm here,' said Muller, brushing his eyes and glancing at the inspector, who folded his arms across his great paunch, 'and I'm here because people are afraid. Or perhaps I should say that most people are content or apathetic and the rest are afraid. Understandably.'

The inspector smiled.

'And so it doesn't matter – or not to me. Living in compartments, with a sort of strictly divided public and personal life, seems wrong if one or other leads to no effort to improve things. I know' – Muller's voice was hoarse and his temples were painful again with a dragging, gnawing sort of ache – 'that most people can't improve things, and don't want to. Most people can only follow, if that. But they'll get no lead from the associates of evil – officials with lush jobs who tuck themselves away in the evenings with pretty pictures and nostalgic music.'

The inspector sighed. He sat for a moment breathing contemplatively. 'It could be a lead, couldn't it? But you're so incredibly naïve – and stupid or courageous – that I don't know what to say.' He sighed again. 'A lot of this could be the result of tucking *yourself* away with too many books for too long.'

'That's your diagnosis?' asked Muller.

'I don't think so. No. You're unusual. Oddly unusual. Dangerously unusual.'

'And I haven't – like everyone else – read widely for years,' said Muller. 'And I'm unlikely to have too many books again.'

'No,' admitted the inspector. 'No. Your property has been destroyed.'

Muller laughed. 'Only my property?'

The inspector shrugged. It was a grotesque movement, extending to his belly, which seemed to wobble slightly.

'You're destroying yourself. Helped by us I daresay, but nothing is certain, Muller. We may – just in time – pull you back.'

'Pull me back?' Muller echoed. 'How? Why?'

The inspector shrugged again. 'Why? News of you is spreading. You're beginning to interest some of the younger people.'

Muller stared. 'Younger people.'

'Intellectuals.' The inspector sighed gently. 'I'm not stating an absolutely solid fact. Such things are – what shall we say? – nebulous. But young people always believe in the present if the present's progressive. Officially,' said the inspector, 'this is the age of perfection, and things – as you term them – can't be improved. But they can be analysed and re-aligned.'

'So I'm open to perfection,' said Muller. 'But these young people. Do they watch Kitty One-Eye and things like that?'

'I doubt it.' The inspector yawned. 'One or two of them perhaps. In a detached clinically intellectual manner, of course. Personally – pervert and wicked old man that I am – I prefer the soft lights and sweet music brigade.'

'I do too,' Muller said grimly. 'A little natural enthusiasm is a good thing.'

'My view exactly. To watch with bated breath is one thing. To be hypocritical afterwards is another. But most people,' said the inspector, 'have lost the power of natural reaction. Genuine emotion is beyond them.'

Muller laughed. 'I doubt it. The last few days – strangely enough – have given me quite a bit of hope. But I'm sure you're right if –'

The inspector's secretary entered abruptly and Muller broke off. The inspector listened as the police girl whispered into his ear. Then he glanced at Muller and touched a bell. Two guards appeared.

'Put the prisoner to bed and attend to him.' The police girl averted her head as the guards moved forward and Muller stood up. 'Tomorrow night, Muller, we'll see if we can recapture a little of that genuine emotion or whatever it is. I hope you'll still hope.'

*

The hall was cone-shaped, the stage being at the point of the cone and the auditorium soaring in segments so contrastingly and startlingly coloured that Muller – waiting with the guards at the edge of the stage – dropped his eyes quickly and concentrated on the business of remaining on his feet. It took quite an effort, and the murmuring, tide-like hum from above of the auditorium filling up, after an initial, barely felt twinge of apprehension, only added to his torpidity.

After the injection he had known nothing. When he came round he still felt drugged; he moved slowly and with difficulty and his breathing seemed constricted. He sat down heavily and the guards gave him a large pot of coffee-like stuff. It was hot and acrid but Muller drank it thirstily. Although hardly – as the inspector had promised – feeling 'fit and strong and ready for battle' he was calm, without fear, and his appetite was surprising. He quickly devoured a substantial meat dish, then he sat for quite a long time, feeling mentally torpid, but with his breathing – surprisingly again – much easier, and an intoxicating strength exciting his middle. Doped, Muller told himself hazily; the dope's doped and the food's doped and the drink's doped. He wondered if poor old Kitty One-Eye was having the same treatment.

After a while the guards roused him and he had a shower, from which he emerged with a sense of well-being, but mentally he was still woolly, and he moved as though in slow motion. The lethargy became almost a loss of identity as, clad only in a short white dressing gown, he stood waiting in the wings of the theatre. He felt duller and hazier until his head nodded; a guard prodded him sharply, and for several minutes he stood bemusedly, no more certain of anything than a drunk stirring in his sleep. At first he couldn't think at all, and he had quite forgotten what he was doing there; the guards shook him violently, and he stood holding his head. 'Love,' he mumbled at last. 'Don't worry,' said one of the guards; 'they'll liven you up.'

The attendants arrived and the depressed-looking doctor. Someone removed Muller's dressing-gown and he was led towards the settee near the centre of the stage. The settee was an oddly shaped, transparent affair; suspended above it, scarcely visible, was a metallic thing, something like a pair of giant calipers: near the settee was a cabinet on a gleaming metal trolley. A twinge of apprehension pierced Muller's muzziness. The caliper thing, obviously enough, would grip and seesaw his behind if he tried to disengage, or if he lacked vigour. 'Vigour,' thought Muller; 'they think of everything; I shouldn't lack that.' The audience quietened as the doctor and attendants fussed busily. An appliance similar to the one used previously was clipped round him, and the doctor – frowning a little – gave him one injection and another. After the second Muller's feeling of half-asphyxiated woolliness was transformed abruptly: he shivered violently as a cold wind seemed to hit him. He might have been young, a young man ski-ing down a mountain with pretty girls watching him. The doctor murmured his satisfaction. 'Feel livelier, eh? Good. A woman's role is important but the man has to do most of –'

A shriek interrupted him, and the audience – quietly watching Muller – gasped as a screaming tornado burst on stage, scattering Muller and his attendants, and dislodging the leads attached to the cabinet. Muller and the doctor jumped, and the fat inspector – pouring sweat – leapt to avoid the blue flash and pursued Kitty and her attendants.

Stark naked, four men trying to hold her, One-Eyed Kate circled the stage, scorn and abuse pouring from her. 'You scum!' she shrieked. 'Trash! Filth! Swine! Doin' this to a decent old woman!' She twirled, ducked, darted from her escort, then – with a sort of pirouette –

stood and beat her leathery old breast. 'For years an' years I've bin a clean, decent, God-fearin' woman, an' if you think you 'orrible rat-spawned riffy-souled melts will –'

The men pounced and grabbed her. 'Now Kit,' panted the inspector. 'Kit –' A chubby foot lashed out and the inspector gasped. The doctor (rather tentatively) stepped forward, but the inspector, holding his groin with one hand, raised the other savagely: Kate ducked and twisted, and, as the men holding her moved to avoid the blow, tore herself free. The audience began to titter, and the titter – as Kate ran round and round the stage, with the attendants in pursuit – swelled to a roar.

Muller watched. At first sight the old woman had horrified him. Her hair was greyish-green and her largish nose red: the rest of her face, thin and shrivelled, was a dirty yellow, made the more loathsome by the glaring white of her sightless eye. Her neck, oddly enough, was quite pale and smooth, but her body, wrinkled and wasted, except for her thighs, was a speckled liverish brown, and dirty grey hair tufted her belly. Muller shuddered; make love to *that*? But admiration and excitement rose in him as the old woman – her sightless eye glaring, scorn and defiance pouring from her – eluded her pursuers again and again, helped if anything by the awkward run she had to adopt because of her toe-less foot.

'Coppers!' she shrieked. 'You couldn't catch cold! Couldn't catch a rabbit! Remember rabbits? You boiled 'em. Put 'em in a pot an' –'

The audience roared and applauded, and the inspector – gasping and dangerously red – bumped into the doctor, who bumped into Muller. 'Don't just *stand* there,' snarled the inspector. 'Give her a jab. Put her out.'

'Men!' screamed Kate. 'Call yourselves *men*!' (One of them, a particularly tall and thin attendant, dived at her, but Kate, with a sort of sideslipping stumble, left him sprawling on the floor, and was away, with her zigzagging hoppity canter). 'Men!' she shrieked. 'Look at 'em! The bloody cowin' age o' shittin' scientific perfection an' not one with a prick worth a tap pipe!'

The audience went wild, and everybody on stage – Muller and the inspector excepted – made a concerted rush at Kate. The old woman hopped on to the settee, and over it. Two of the attendants crashed into it, and the very tall one, trying another flying tackle, missed Kate by a yard, and crashed into the doctor. That gentleman was not amused, and neither was the inspector. 'Stand still!' he roared. 'Stop it! Everybody stand STILL!!' The men paused uncertainly, and Kate – hands on her heaving sides – shrieked derisively, her sightless eye seeming to glare with scorn.

'Men!' she screeched. 'Men! When I was a gel men loved me an' paid to love me, an' they *was* men then an' the only good thing about 'em *then* was their money. Money,' shrieked Kate. 'Money! But money's 'ad nothin' to do with it for a long time now 'cause I'm decent afore God with money to spare, an' no erpology for a man's shamed *me* without payin' for it – payin' for it! – an' before I leave here I'll –'

The inspector, quietly and slowly, advanced on Kate, and took her arm. She didn't resist – or seem to know that her arm was being held and the doctor approached quickly with a syringe.

'Kate,' said the inspector.

The sightless eye was turned towards him. ''Ossradish Charlie. In the old days it was a quid or a bit o' that when you felt like it or in you'd go for solicitin'. Wapsaw,' jeered Kate, 'was always as clean as its coppers.'

'Now Kate,' said the inspector, as the doctor raised his syringe.

'An eye,' cried the old woman, 'for an eye! A tooth for a tooth an' 'ere's a gift from One-Eyed Kate.' And with her free hand she grabbed the syringe and plunged it into the doctor's face.

The doctor screamed with pain and terror. Holding his eye (which the needle seemed to have punctured) he staggered away; in an instant the stage was full of big, blue-uniformed men. Muller, very naked and puny in such company, moved his feet jerkily to avoid the jackboots.

For a moment there was uproar, then there was silence, abrupt and frightening. The guards melted away and the audience scarcely breathed as Jallen strode on stage.

Jallen looked about him, and paused. His face was terrible, his voice metallic and curiously controlled. 'Not a very successful evening, Veale.'

The inspector licked his lips. 'No sir.'

'Not well conceived or planned.'

The inspector's face was ashen.

'And we've lost a doctor and a prostitute.'

'Yes sir.'

'The prostitute was the more resourceful and efficient.'

The inspector licked his lips again, and Jallen surveyed Muller for a full half-minute, before glancing at the audience, and considering the inspector. 'So which is the greater loss, and is the Committee wise?'

'Yes sir.'

'And it's always possible to lose something else. Think about it, Veale – before seeing me in the morning.' Jallen spoke in little more than a murmur, and the silence was deathly as he strode away.

Chapter 6

On Monday morning – the sun was bright: far out on the square guards were drilling – Muller descended to his office feeling like a sick and ageing man who has walked ten miles. Not, of course, that such a man would walk ten miles, but Muller's exhaustion was so acute that it took a considerable effort to speak. Even his escort was sympathetic.

'You look ninety,' said the guard.

'Feel it.'

'Not,' said the guard, as they approached the lift, 'that you'll see ninety. So don't worry. And if you feel barmy they all go barmy so there's no need to worry about that either. With any luck they'll put you out of your misery.'

'Can't wait,' said Muller.

The guard yawned, and they sank rapidly. 'You've been dead jammy so far. Way they've got it in for you it looked a dead cert for the old Tapthywhatsit treatment.'

'Lucky,' mumbled Muller. 'Always.'

His left leg felt cramped and his right foot was dead. Slowly he hobbled towards the office. Most of the guards who passed grinned. 'An' it never happened!' one of them jeered.

*

No. It never happened. And it couldn't have been worse if it had. When they returned him to his room – if it could be called a room – Muller had suffered the worst night of his life. For the first few hours he lay on his side, his mouth an inch or so open; he couldn't move and his breath came in uneven gasps. It seemed an actual rather than a hysterical paralysis, but Muller's mind was acutely disordered.

Many times in his life he had – because of a disappointment, a quarrel, a setback in love – been badly upset, and because he was emotional and not well-integrated, he had always suffered sharply. For hours he had tossed and turned, every word that had been said or written pouring again and again through his mind. After two hours or so of that he would become a little calmer, and (because he was a dreamer) rearrange the scene to something more to his liking, and at last drop off to sleep. It was childish, of course, and when he awoke make-believe was no good at all – it couldn't and didn't help, and there was the day and work to be faced. As he grew older he turned to sedatives, which on the whole he used sensibly, and, as he grew older, he became somewhat more balanced emotionally. The sedatives, with other treatment, would have benefited him more in his youth, when he was completely at the mercy of his emotions, but even then, nothing that had upset him was revised except at his will. In his imagination he could make a failure a success, he could change anything he disliked to something likeable; but what had happened remained what had happened. And when he went to bed he could hear and see all too clearly. The scene or incident that had upset him wasn't distorted; it was repeated too often and too quickly. The pain and hazard lay in the uncontrollable repetition.

But Muller, after they had half-carried him from the hall and dropped him on his bed, lay for hours in a state of physical paralysis and mental delirium. He couldn't move and he couldn't close his mouth. Spittle dribbled from it and ran down his jaw and neck. He knew about that, he could feel it, but he couldn't close his mouth and he was unable to think about anything that had happened in the hall. His eyes were open a little but the glare of the lights didn't trouble him. The background was dark but every second images flashed before him. Each image was different and each was terrible. There were people he had never seen, men and women with loathsome expressions and vile deformities, grotesque animals and creatures too foul for a book. With lightning rapidity – like an album flipped rapidly – they flashed before his eyes with a clarity possible only to madness.

If Muller had been able to reason he might have told himself that his derangement was a worsening of his former state of mind, but he wasn't able to reason, and his mind, in the most excitable years of his youth, had known nothing like this. And it wasn't merely that he was in the grip of fantasy or delirium but – aware of his terror, very briefly now and then aware of his danger – that he was helpless before a bombardment of evil that would destroy him for ever. The bombardment seemed deliberate, the visions came quicker until his mind was almost totally possessed. His only shield was a remnant of his former capacity, a part of his mind that – frailly and ineffectively – tried to catch the visions and hurl them away. But make-believe, transforming demons into angels, was no more possible now than flies in August. Helpless, unable to fight, Muller's respiration increased until steam rose from the sweat-soaked bed. Towards four in the morning two guards peering down from the roof could barely see him.

'The hell,' said one. 'What is it?'

'Condensation I suppose,' shrugged the other. 'Better go look.' They went down to Muller's glass prison and stared at him. After a time they called their sergeant, who called the duty doctor.

'Drugs and overstrain, I suppose,' said the latter. 'But why call me?'

'That's what I said,' frowned the sergeant. 'Why call me?'

The guards shifted uneasily. 'Well,' said one, 'we didn't know what to do. We didn't know if there was a responsibility in this case.'

The doctor looked frightened. 'Responsibility? Not for me!'

Muller didn't know what was happening, but there were grey shadows, blurs and a faint humming that touched something in his brain. He tried to move and groaned.

'Will he live?' asked the sergeant.

'Might,' shrugged the doctor. 'Die or go mad more probably. Isn't that what usually happens?'

'Yes sir,' said one of the guards. 'But we don't know what's wanted in this case, and we daren't ask.'

The sergeant cleared his throat. 'It's no use going higher up for orders. They wouldn't touch it. Don't know what's wanted you see.'

'Only Mr Jallen, sir,' said the guard. 'And who'd ask him?'

The four men moved uneasily.

'Point is, somebody has to take it,' said the sergeant. 'And you know what happened last night. This man would have gone then if Mr Jallen had intended it.'

The doctor thought for a moment. 'All right. I'll try something.'

When they left him Muller lay as still as before. He wasn't asleep but his consciousness was fractional. The visions were still with him but far less acutely. Every moment or so one floated down gently, wavered before him, and vanished. Muller – without realizing it – began to frown slightly, and his throat muscles moved as though he were swallowing something. Ease ebbed through his body and the horrible rasp of his breathing ceased. The duty doctor, listening in his office, sat back as Muller's pulse and respiration fell steadily.

The doctor sat thinking and his patient slept. When Muller awoke it was Sunday afternoon and the sun was brilliant. He felt normal, hazily, dreamily, beautifully calm – much as he had felt years ago on Sunday morning. Yawning he had padded downstairs, but, after a bath and cup of tea he was full of vitality, tidying the room and tackling the week's correspondence before his father came downstairs.

'You do make such a noise,' his father grumbled.

Muller turned over again and slept. He began to dream, of a road, a long, wide road that went on and on. Again and again he saw the road, and each time he was roaring along it.

*

The manager gave him a quick look but said nothing, and for the first two hours Muller sat almost completely still. His breathing was laboured and he felt quite heavily drugged again. I have almost certainly had it, he thought hazily, but better make some display of willingness. Occasionally he touched his head – as though thinking – with his left hand, and moved the pen a little with his right, but the manager might have been miles away. Muller – slowly and laboriously – turned to look at him once or twice, but the manager's back remained solidly and cautiously indifferent. 'Bad sign,' thought Muller; 'bad sign.'

Towards lunchtime he felt a little better, and though the meal itself – a sort of treacly stew – was repulsive it at least put something into his middle. In the degradation of Cell 97 Muller sat awkwardly with his legs twisted as though gripping a pole, but he – somewhat perversely – began to feel more human. Years ago he had accused a pretty graduate of the Wapsaw Higher School of being a social butterfly, and 'I love you in a sort of way', she had written, 'but if I wasn't a butterfly I'd become a drugge.' Muller began to feel less of a drugge. On the way back to the office he walked slowly, but the paralysing cramps were much less severe and his breathing was near normal.

He worked steadily for a time, then (it might have been planned: he was completely out of record sheets) set off along the passage. It was odd: the place was now familiar but he felt as though he had been away for a long time. Gingerly he edged through the machine shop and his heart and step quickened as he approached Mr Edkins; but he was disappointed. The little man looked startled, surprised – and considerably apprehensive.

'Here,' he said, producing a sheaf of papers. 'Take these and hop it.'

Muller stared. 'What's the matter?'

'Nothing,' Mr Edkins said nervously, his eyes all over the place. 'But don't hang about here.'

Muller frowned. 'Didn't you expect to see me again after Saturday night?'

'No,' said Mr Edkins. 'Yes. I mean – now look. Have you seen yourself? It's out of the question. You'll have to put it off for a few days.'

'May be too late.'

'I know. But I can't help it.'

'Mr Edkins,' said Muller, 'what's gone wrong? What is it?'

The little man stared at his desk and spoke rapidly. 'I don't know. Only rumours. It's the other night. Jallen. Inefficiency and his department ridiculed. Thinks you're infective and your contacts dubious. They're under arrest.'

Muller glanced up and down the shop. Everything seemed normal. The usual guard lounged near the lift; at the lower end of the shop there were guards in plenty, but their behaviour seemed casual.

'Infective?' he said.

'Spread doubt – discontent. And,' said Mr Edkins, 'don't be deceived. It's hopeless.'

'Yes,' said Muller. 'My contacts. What do you mean?'

'Everybody who's seen you – interviewed you. When a thing goes as wrong as that Jallen suspects babes unborn.'

'No use blaming an old prostitute?'

'Too simple. Now for God's sake take these and hop it. The way things are I'm not –' Mr Edkins stopped abruptly and stared. He stared hard. Then he lost the battle with himself and bent over his desk.

Muller had walked thirty or forty yards on his way back to the office when he saw McAllister approaching. Muller's reactions were faulty. He stopped dead, stood for a second, stepped forward and signalled with his eyes. All he could think of was the passage leading to the pattern shop. Perhaps they could (if only for a moment, if only to say good-bye) talk there.

But McAllister – grim, horribly emaciated – remained amazingly poised and calm. He waved his sheaf of papers, and Muller (legs rubbery, heart thumping) turned and followed him. McAllister veered to the left, walking boldly towards the guard. Muller glanced across at Mr Edkins: the little man, mouth open, was standing petrified.

'Press the button five seconds after I start talking to the guard,' said McAllister.

They were within ten yards of the guard before he saw them. The guard – tall, surly, bored – frowned, but he was more curious than suspicious.

McAllister waved his papers and said: 'The Process Inspector says will you take these up to the Director's office.'

The guard stared – at McAllister, the papers, and back at McAllister.

'The Director's office?' he said. 'The *Director's* office?'

'The order's there,' said McAllister prodding the sheets. The guard blinked rapidly and McAllister's left hand opened. In it was a tiny pistol with a point like a needle. The door of the lift opened and the guard turned sharply. As he did so McAllister pressed the trigger. There was a smell of burning and the guard gave a sort of jerk and gurgled. Before he could fall McAllister had him into the lift.

Muller's mouth was dry and his legs were shaking. He glanced down at the guard. The man was dead; his face was purple and froth was around his lips.

'Haven't long,' gasped McAllister, yanking at his trousers. Around one leg was a roll of flex attached to two small metal objects. 'Only Edkins saw us I think. He'll give the alarm – bound to. Whether he'll have the guts to wait a few minutes I don't know.'

The flex dropped beside the dead guard, and McAllister hoisted his trousers as the lift shot upwards.

It was superbly incredible or (Muller thought later), incredibly superb. McAllister, papers in one hand again, pistol in the other, stood waiting; he held himself more erect than usual but he was breathing heavily, and his pallor, emphasized by the spots of red on his sunken cheeks, was corpse-like.

The lift stopped and the gates opened. A guard – burly and elderly – was seated across the passage opposite the lift. McAllister – smiling, one hand behind his back, the other waving the papers – stepped forward and said: 'The Process Inspector leaves things lying about. Careless man.'

The guard's look of profound, almost stupefied disbelief changed to alarm, and he jumped up, but McAllister had pressed the trigger. The passage was narrow; McAllister grabbed the falling guard and with a swing heaved him into the lift. There was a considerable thump; in alarm Muller hurried into the passage but his anxiety changed at once to amazement; the gates closed and the lift had descended again.

The passage was short – forty feet or so – as well as narrow, and it ended in a blank wall. Muller's legs twitched as he tried to run and tried not to run. Finally he tiptoed up the passage and peered round the corner. There were doors to offices with a sort of porter's enclosure in the distance and two guards standing near it. As one of them turned Muller withdrew sharply. He stood for a moment in complete indecision, then walked back to the lift.

Staring at the gates he wondered if McAllister had gone mad. Had he – more probably – collapsed and in falling touched the lift button; or had he (not that it seemed possible) gone down again to see Edkins or to attempt to rescue other prisoners? For another moment Muller stared desperately, then the gates opened and the lift was back, but only four feet or so above the level of the passage. McAllister threw out two lengths of wire, then Muller grabbed his arms and helped him scramble out of the lift.

For a moment both men stood breathing heavily. McAllister's shoulders heaved and Muller's mouth was still asphyxiatingly dry but he was sweating freely. He tried to speak, but couldn't, and stared stupidly when McAllister indicated the roof of the lift. 'Jimmy,' said McAllister, and with a hand under Muller's crutch hoisted him on to the roof of the lift. With his ears pinging and lights flashing before his eyes Muller lay semi-conscious as McAllister – kneeling beside him – worked feverishly on the lift's tiny power unit. After a few minutes the outer door of the lift closed. McAllister lay flat and the lift glided up to floor level. McAllister was still fumbling away in the dark when sirens started to shriek. Up in the lift shaft they sounded like sad trumpets heard from a long way off.

'Edkins is a hero,' breathed McAllister. 'Given us ten minutes at least.'

Muller stirred but McAllister held him down. 'Don't sit up. You'll be crushed.'

'The wires,' panted Muller. 'The wires down in the lift.'

'The wires are up here,' said McAllister. 'So are we. Now listen Jimmy. You see my plan. I thought we couldn't get out of the building and couldn't stay in it – place will really be gone over and we'd have been rooted out if we'd managed to conceal ourselves. But when and if they can't find us they'll think –'

McAllister stopped. Very little could be heard. Only a faint sort of shuffle, then silence again. 'Office guard probably,' McAllister said softly. 'Horror at finding the dead men. Now things will happen.'

They did. There were footsteps and voices – excited but strangely muted – and the lift quivered. There were other voices, much sharper, and a very loud voice; then silence as the lift sank rapidly. After two or three minutes it rose again. It was quite a small lift, almost entirely silent in movement, but Muller, lying close to McAllister with his feet well away from the shaft wall, could hear little except his friend's breathing.

Twice more the lift repeated its journey. There was, perhaps because of the total darkness, little sense of movement, but McAllister – to Muller's surprise – gave a sudden heave and was violently sick. McAllister had always been much the stronger and least neurotic of the two, and Muller, losing some of his fear, was almost enjoying the travel. It was cool in the lift shaft and the air displacement was particularly pleasing. Muller breathed deeply: it was like living again.

'Feeling better?' he asked, but the lift trembled sharply – almost ominously – as several large men strode into it with an order snapped in a voice that could be heard very clearly. It was impossible to mistake it: Jallen had arrived on the scene.

For about ten minutes the lift stayed at the machine shop level. Muller lay rigidly, straining his ears, but could hear nothing except the distant machines. When the lift rose again he moved his head dangerously near the shaft wall, and heard Jallen – as the lift stopped and opened – snarl: 'Accomplices? Of course they had accomplices. Waiting here by the lift with a change of clothing and false papers probably. But,' he snapped, 'it would take more than that to get them through. Muller particularly has a face like a corpse. *That* face wouldn't get far.'

Jallen's voice faded as his party moved off. After a time McAllister – very slowly and carefully – began soaking up the vomit with the upper part of his clothing. An hour or more passed and Muller had heard nothing. He turned over, wondering what would happen when Jallen had satisfied himself that they weren't hiding in the offices or anywhere else in the building. Everything and everybody would be taken to pieces and many lives would be endangered. 'Mac,' said Muller, but McAllister – naked to the waist – stared silently into the darkness. Muller moved restlessly and turned over again. It was cold and the unrelieved darkness didn't lessen the feeling of imprisonment. He pillowed his arms under his head and thought of the many nights when he had longed for sleep. The more one ached for it the more unattainable it became. Muller wondered if he would ever sleep again, and sleep in a bed. It was unlikely. McAllister and he, within a few hours or a day or so at the most, were almost certain to die. And death, even now, wasn't an easy question to face. How lovely it must have been, thought Muller, to have lived years ago, to have slept easily and naturally and to have walked out into the morning air with birds singing. He sighed; birds singing and the sun shining on trees and fields. Even in the great cities there had been flowers and open spaces and stretches of water. 'How lovely,' thought Muller, 'to have lain in grass on a warm summer's day and to have dozed for an hour.' He sighed; and, on the lift roof, in the chilly blackness, slept.

*

McAllister watched his friend. Sleeping like a babe. Poor old bastard. The poor daft old bastard. They'd certainly put him through it. And there was no point in going on, no point at all. Their chances of escape were minute, and of survival, nil. Further suffering was pointless, and the most sensible thing would be to end it now. McAllister touched the tiny power unit that lay between him and Muller and wondered if education wasn't at the root of it all. 'I was a fool,' he told himself, 'a stupid damn fool not to have gone meekly to Banff'; things might have been tolerable there with a vestige of nonconformity and pleasant girls not too well indoctrinated. It was possible but not too probable; Banff had been a fishing village or market town or something of the sort, but now it was probably an antiseptic settlement with one or two glacial caverns jammed with guards and prisoners – and a few children – going mad with tension and boredom.

McAllister writhed and turned sharply. Propping himself up with his right hand he scuffed the back of his neck with the other, massaging violently with his fingertips until he was breathless and his stomach ached. It was cold, damn cold, and some simple dead-as-the-dodo thing like pneumonia would supervene if they stayed up here long. The machine shop and offices had suffered from a dry, airless sort of heat, and the remedial extensions had been stifling. Muller, weak-chested and soaked in drugs, would be particularly susceptible.

McAllister glanced at his friend and smashed his clenched fist against the roof of the lift. Again he lifted his fist, but it hung in the air. 'Blasted fool,' McAllister told himself. The entombment gave a feeling of complete isolation and safety; it hadn't even occurred to him that he might be heard. McAllister listened intently; if another guard was watching the lift he couldn't be more than twelve feet away. The chances were that the prisoners had been locked up, and that every available guard – together with hundreds called in from outside – were searching the building from top to bottom. Jallen, too, wasn't the man to lock the stable door after the horse had bolted. McAllister's chest heaved. My *God*, but it was strange. The animal world had long ceased to exist, but the language was still littered with four-legged associations. They didn't like it, of course, and they had tried to stop it; the common room had often been discomfited with McAllister's sarcasm.

His chest heaving, McAllister stared grimly into the darkness. Blaming poor old Muller, and he was here probably because the cat no longer sat on the mat and the cow couldn't jump over the moon. Seemed absurd, of course, even symbolically. Years ago a lift attendant hearing noises from a lift shaft might have thought what? Not of political prisoners if there weren't any, and not of animals unlikely to be found in lift shafts. But if the lift worked perfectly and if the wind (and what lift attendant would think of *wind*?) wasn't blowing down the shaft might he think not of bats in the belfry but of rats in the shaft? McAllister's strong teeth gleamed for a moment and he rubbed his bare chest violently. On one occasion Miss Cherholm (pure science and a Committee informant if ever there was one) had not only denied all knowledge of animals but denied that animals had ever existed. McAllister had made a model of a rat and placed it in her desk; she had screamed her head off.

McAllister's chest heaved. There was fear of the known, fear of the unknown, and fear. And there was association, association of ideas and the weakest and most human thing of all: the attachment to the familiar. That's what the planners had destroyed, or tried to destroy, attachment to the past and to familiar things. It wasn't easy, of course, with older people, and not too easy with children. The authorities concentrated on them, obviously, and a child, of course, had little to go on in the way of memory. But where did memory end and instinct begin? Instinct perhaps was strongest in women but little girls for a considerable period hadn't been allowed to play with dolls.

McAllister took a long slow breath and gently massaged his aching stomach. He was no expert, but primary education seventy or eighty years ago had started with spelling, and the sentimental associations must have been considerable. The poor little sods had to agree that one plus one made two, certainly, and it wasn't too difficult for many of them to identify C-A-T with Tiddles and D-O-G with Bonzo. Not that all children, of course, had a cat or a dog – or a horse or a cow – but most children had seen one, and teacher was usually handy at drawing. Visual aids became popular, particularly when progress and the spread of education made spelling more difficult.

McAllister began to breathe more quickly. There it was. Education began with the familiar. It may not have seemed so, particularly to the kids starting school, but it was a sort of natural development. What it led to was another matter. It had led to the destruction of a large part of the world and its people. But that, McAllister almost cried, wasn't the fault of education generally and of the little kids starting school. And it wasn't easy for the Secretariat after the nuclear war. Because of the madness of the scientists little was left in nature. Foreign languages went overboard, overseas journeys, trips to the countryside. Out went the majority of physical and mental contacts. A whole mass of literature became useless and undesirable. There had to be a new start, and the science that had destroyed demanded total allegiance. The promise was perfection and the weapon was fear. A child, said the Secretariat, is an empty vessel; we will fill the vessel.

Remnants of the past were scanty, but a few people had managed to preserve family relics, and McAllister had seen two or three children's exercise books of long ago. They were (to him) heartbreaking things, though his colleagues would have been the last to believe it. Most of them thought him excessively worldly; the suave cynic of nearly forty who had been the slick wisecracker of thirty and the lean refuter of twenty. He made one or two of them just a little uncomfortable. By his manner, something about him, you could sense that he didn't believe in *anything*. But he had conformed, he was efficient. And he was hard. McAllister, they would have agreed, was the opposite of sloppy. McAllister's colleagues laughed rarely, and McAllister's reaction to ancient exercise books wouldn't have amused them. Another of his jokes, they would have thought; they wouldn't have believed it. But McAllister found the crude essays and crayon drawings strangely moving. Simple, pretty little things. They had every fault under the sun; but they were childlike and natural.

But now, said the Secretariat, a child is an empty vessel; he must come to us empty and undecorated. There must be no toys or amusements, no fairy tales or stories. And this education began at the age of four and a child made no contact with professional teachers until he was six. Many children, it was true, had recovered by the time they were nine, and most of them were normal (acceptable to the authorities) by the time they were eleven. But they weren't children. The most difficult thing was their silence. Children, surely, had always been naturally loquacious, but it was hell now getting them to talk. McAllister (unlike the authorities and a majority of his profession) doubted the ideological effects of the almost permanent silence. At times it was unnerving; bad in many ways for teacher and pupils; and although there was nothing to prevent the kids from letting rip when they weren't at school they rarely did so, because of their training.

McAllister sat up carefully, and rubbed his back. It was like a slab of ice. After rubbing away for a few minutes he readjusted his soiled clothing (which he had wrapped round the lift's power unit) and was nearly sick again. The smell made him heave, but McAllister took a huge breath and managed to control himself. Hadn't been like this for years. Behaving like a daft kid. But that was the point. The kids never *were* sick; they didn't do it in their pants; they didn't cry. All that was stopped shortly after they started school. Naked, said the dictators, you came into the world, and naked you'll come to school. School, said the authorities, is the first contact with reality; a child of four, said the authorities, may have seen people killed, and killed horribly, but that, to a child, isn't reality; it's fantasy. School, however, was reality and nudity helped. Nudity was reality; nudity was equality. ('It also gives a feeling of helplessness, in certain circumstances,' McAllister had said once. 'Just the sort of thing to appeal to our rulers.')

The Primary Developments Wings were certainly successful. The idea, of course, was that infantile emotions and instincts were of little use to the child or community; it was best to destroy them at the roots; in difficult cases they might return, but the child would be older with the equipment to handle them. In the blackness of the lift shaft McAllister almost laughed. Would Muller and he be here now if they had been primarily developed? Possibly not. Possibly not, McAllister muttered under his breath.

Officialdom was proud of the P.D.W.s, but only official parties of visitors were permitted. McAllister's inclusion in a semi-official party (of two) wouldn't have been possible but for a brief affair with a P.D.W. executive; a surprising lady who specialized in reactival didacticism for six-year-olds. There were about a dozen children in each class. Each child – widely separated from his neighbour – sat silent and still, a prisoner of the ditrabionic apparatus clipped to his head. McAllister at first was sickened by the nudity. It was pointless, a typical bit of nastiness. But, after a few minutes, he forgot it. Clothing, no matter how uniform, would give some sort of identity – or humanity –

and the most horrifying thing was the similarity. Each child might have been a statue, and the same statue. Featureless, motionless, as anonymous as the utter silence, they comprised an exhibition in depravity and subjection that almost unnerved McAllister. He felt an urge to shout, to do something, but he controlled himself, and muttered darkly about Jack and Jill.

'I don't see the point,' murmured his companion.

'I don't think I do,' McAllister said grimly.

His friend frowned. 'Few people nowadays are familiar with the old nursery rhymes. But you shouldn't quote them. You might be misunderstood.'

'I might be,' said McAllister.

They paused in a corridor, and the woman hesitated. 'You're oddly impressionable. And you lack objectivity. But . . . let's try again. Look closely at the beginners and then go straight to the children due to leave. You may see a difference.'

'I've seen it,' snapped McAllister. 'One four-year-old was almost recognizable as a child – there was a trace of bewilderment and fear – but the five-, six- and seven-year-olds lacked all signs of life. Is that the difference?'

'We'd better go,' the woman said sharply, and McAllister went. For days he was confused; nauseated and reactionary on the one hand and mentally uncertain on the other. The P.D.W.s were a fairly recent innovation and it was early to pass judgement. God alone knew what the future would be, and the children had to live in the future. They had been ruthlessly disciplined scientifically, but it was true that personality faults were rare. Few became delinquents. Fewer went mad. They were extremely healthy and illness or natural death in childhood was almost unknown. But very few after their conditioning remained childlike; they had few feelings of childhood; they weren't adult but they weren't children. At times as McAllister faced his silent, expressionless class he felt that they were scarcely human.

Now for God's sake, McAllister told himself. There's

nothing you can do. It's evil but so is society and so is the world or what's left of it. And the evil was inevitable. After years of horror it was inescapable. So was dehumanization. So was experiment. McAllister could – he told himself – accept most things, but the P.D.W.s did something to him. You're being perverse, he told himself, perverse, illogical and stupid. You're not particularly fond of children and the kids' parents hadn't the guts to raise a whisper. If parents couldn't fight for their kids things were hopeless anyway. Things *were* hopeless, so it was pointless saying anything. It was pointless and dangerous. I'll say nothing, McAllister told himself, but his reaction was characteristic. Irritable and intolerant, he went about for days in a tearing hurry. When he spoke he snapped, and although he managed to avoid any direct reference to the P.D.W.s he put several of his colleagues' noses so badly out of joint that a carpeting was inevitable. 'McAllister,' said the Deputy Head, 'you've been going about like an executioner with urgent duties to perform. All of us feel like that occasionally but you've gone too far. I don't know what's eating you but you seem to need treatment. Possibly even re-classification.'

McAllister checked himself. For years he had thought himself secure. And re-classification could mean disaster and meant demotion at the least. He stared at the Deputy Head, who said, 'You've always been a little too audaciously self-assured.'

'Audaciously!' echoed McAllister. 'Assured perhaps but not audaciously. I doubt if it would be possible.' He paused. 'I'm dependable and you know it, and I'm not too stodgy. It's difficult at times to avoid a false impression, but my work, for instance. Isn't that satisfactory?'

'There's more to life than work,' said the Deputy Head.

'I'm glad to hear it,' said McAllister. 'But all it amounts to I suppose is that I speak a little too sharply at times. My tongue must get the better of me.'

'It won't get the better of *me*,' said the Deputy Head.

Taut as a lathe, McAllister stared tensely. 'I didn't think

any difficult questions were raised,' he said at last. 'But yours is the power.'

The Deputy Head smiled a little. 'Yes. Mine is the power. It can send people up, McAllister. Up *or* down.'

Up or down. McAllister remembered the words as he lay in the lift shaft.

*

Muller awoke with a start, sitting up abruptly and banging his head. The confusion he often felt on awakening had seldom been so quickly dispelled. Startled, he fell back and turned over – bumping into McAllister, who growled promptly; 'Bloody fool. Told you to mind your head.'

Muller rubbed his streaming eyes. 'Asleep,' he mumbled.

'Asleep!' scoffed McAllister. 'Don't mention insomnia to me again.'

As his head and the pain cleared Muller started to shiver. It was cold, clammily cold. Rubbing his hands together he asked McAllister what time he thought it was.

'How do I know?' grunted McAllister. 'Past midnight I'd say. 'Bout one or two a.m.'

'Two a.m.!' echoed Muller. 'Can't be surely?'

'Don't know about surely,' McAllister retorted. 'You were asleep a good three hours before I dozed off. At a guess I was asleep two or three hours and it's two or three hours since I awoke. That puts the time at anything between 11 p.m. and 2 a.m.'

Muller waited. Despair was inevitable, but McAllister seemed more peeved than anything. 'I've been sleeping off the dope I suppose,' Muller said at last. 'There is that feel of 2 a.m. Couldn't we get out now, Neil?'

'Get out to *what*?' McAllister almost snarled. 'To a speedy and certain death? Don't be idiotic.' Breathing heavily, he was silent for a moment. 'Sorry,' he said more calmly. 'I'm beginning to stretch. Hope I don't snap.' After another silence he said, 'We have no chance, Jim, you must realize that. Our escape is little more than a gesture. Or a bit of realism if you like. Suffering two or three days of misery in order to avoid weeks or months of torture. But,' said McAllister, 'we'll give them a run for their money and it's best to wait until this time tomorrow. The block has been thoroughly searched by now and tomorrow it will really be taken apart. After all that they'll be satisfied that we're not in the building.'

'No chance?' said Muller. 'Do you mean we won't get away from here – or from the town?'

'That'll take some doing won't it?' McAllister laughed softly. 'But if we *do* – and we'll need miracles of luck – if we do where do we go? How do we live? What do we eat?'

'I know,' said Muller. 'I know.'

'You don't know,' McAllister snapped irritably. 'You're as unrealistic as ever for all they've done to you.'

Gently – and carefully – Muller sighed. 'Perhaps.'

'There are ruined towns. Dozens of them. If we can swipe a machine and evade masses of men and detection apparatus we may reach one of them. But how would we *eat*?'

'Exactly,' Muller said carefully. Although he had (according to McAllister) been asleep for eight hours he felt as though he hadn't slept for days, and it took quite an effort to speak. 'I thought,' he said diffidently, 'we might have a chance if we could reach the coast.'

'The *coast*?' McAllister demanded, as though Muller were crazy.

'Well,' said Muller, 'so far as we know it hasn't been touched for years. They don't bother about it, I mean. Preserving the coastline and so on.'

'And so on,' McAllister jeered. 'So by and by and so on we'll tuck ourselves away in an old sand dune and eat seaweed. Is that it?'

'It's an idea,' said Muller. 'The sea must be solid with fish and –'

'Inedible. Poisoned, you damn fool,' snapped McAllister.

There was an uncomfortable silence. 'Rocket attacks are becoming more and more sporadic, wouldn't you agree, Neil?' Muller said at last.

'I would. So what? Wasn't there a ban on nuclear tests before most of the world went smack?'

'I know. A stockpile exploded in Russia and –'

'Ancient history,' snapped McAllister. 'Ancient history. What's that to do with us here and now?'

Muller sighed. 'Nothing. But there may be places where we might have more of a chance.'

'Places. Places. Thousands of miles away. The only chance is in a manned rocket. We couldn't do it. There are dozens of security and defence networks to pierce. We couldn't do it without massive collaboration.'

'I suppose not.' Muller hesitated. 'The strange thing is ... the people who've given me hope since this started. The man at the Housing Office, the men who brought me, even –'

'Oh, for God's sake,' McAllister snapped. 'It's always been the same with dictatorships. People don't like them, but doing something about it is another matter. And being a bit pleasant and human to a man who's had it is the worst form of hypocrisy and cowardice. "I hate doing this," they suggest, "fundamentally I'm with you," but they'll feed their fat bellies and lose no sleep at all whilst you're being tortured or killed.'

'But they're under arrest,' Muller protested.

'If they're under arrest they can't help us and we can't help them. We need power. We need the backing of men with power. It's the last thing we'll get.'

Muller thought for a moment. 'You mean we need such backing to revolt. But who nowadays seriously contemplates revolution? Almost nobody. Wouldn't that of itself increase our chances of –'

'No,' snapped McAllister. 'You're off your rocker, which isn't surprising. Think, man. To take over this town would mean smashing five or six scientific lines of defence. How do you think I manipulated this lift?'

'I don't know,' sighed Muller. 'I thought about it. I'm no wiser.'

'Lifts,' said McAllister, 'at one time used a system of

electricity and weights. Balance and counterbalance if you like, but there was direct contact. See what I mean?'

'Yes,' said Muller.

'You don't. But to take a simpler example. When you pressed a light switch you made a contact. The switch moved a bit of metal that touched the live wire. The circuit as they called it, was completed, and the light came on. Electricity. Needed wires and cables and so on.'

'Even I know that,' Muller protested. 'But what's the point?'

'The point is that Eardley's great – oh Christ!' And McAllister made a half-groaning half-snarling noise and thrashed about violently. He was fully clothed again, and although his presence was all too tangible Muller could see little more than the whitish blur of his face. But he edged away a little. 'My guts!' exclaimed McAllister. 'My bloody guts!'

'Couldn't you get the lift down to the machine shop?' Muller asked quietly.

McAllister – breathing heavily – didn't answer, and Muller, after waiting a moment, said: 'I thought we might find something to eat down there.'

McAllister's heavy breathing stopped. There was a silence before he said sourly: 'Oh, thought you'd gone barmy.' There was another silence before he said – almost plaintively – 'The best idea so far. But there's no food down there.'

'I suppose not,' Muller admitted. 'I thought we might find something in the guards' lockers. A good swig of water would be better than nothing.'

McAllister – breathing heavily again – thought it over. 'It's tempting. Another twenty-four hours of this won't do us any good at all. But it's too risky. There may be work parties down there and that means guards.'

Muller doubted if – in the circumstances – work was going on in the machine shop, but he didn't say so. Everything depended on McAllister; without him emergence from the lift shaft would be impossible. Not that it would physically be possible to be without him; mentally it would. Muller had always regarded him as a strong character; he hoped he wasn't the sort of strong character who would give way. 'I suppose you're right,' he said. He waited a moment and added: 'I haven't much technical knowledge, as you know, Neil. What did you mean about Eardley's discovery?'

'Oh,' McAllister said listlessly. 'You know. No wires and cables. Power without pipes. Ethereal power, as some idiot called it.'

'Ethereal,' Muller repeated, shivering violently: almost every particle of him ached. He wondered if something very simple would give the game away. In a few hours' time the working day would start and loud sneezes might well be heard coming from the lift shaft. 'Crazy isn't it?' he said, and McAllister snorted furiously and sat up.

'It's not crazy at all, you idiot! Eardley's discovery was a tremendous advance, but I'm concerned with the implications.'

'Quite,' Muller said hastily. 'I quite see that.'

McAllister made several God-give-me-strength noises. 'Electricity,' he said with measured calm, 'used to be a cumbersome affair of huge generating stations with cables and so on to carry the power. The rockets put paid to most of the stations – and cables – so Eardley's discovery was more than welcomed.'

'Oh, I know,' said Muller. 'But I thought each building generated its own power and so on?'

McAllister sighed lengthily. 'Yes. To some extent. It has to be boosted – from a central point that powers street lighting and whatnot.'

'Oh,' said Muller. 'I see.'

McAllister grunted. 'Wish I could.' He rubbed the nape of his neck. 'But that's the position. Power's airborne now. It flies. It's linked with radio and nuclear charges. They can put rings around the moon and barriers of power around each block. Break the barrier and there's a bang.'

Muller sighed. 'No wonder we need technical help to escape.'

'To revolt. To *revolt*.'

'Yes,' Muller said doubtfully. 'But these impulses – radio, electrical or whatever they are. It's obvious enough. If suspects leave any particular building they'll be destroyed. But surely something could be done about the explosives? And –'

'No!' groaned McAllister. 'God Almighty no! We're talking of extreme measures. Even Jallen wouldn't destroy a whole block unless things were bad. He'd arrest the suspects if he could.'

'If he could?'

'Certainly. And what's to stop him?'

'Nothing. There's no opposition.'

'Exactly. But the deterrent is there – and it's extremely complex, not a simple sort of bomb one can dismantle, you idiot!'

'Oh I know. I know. But –'

'You don't know!' McAllister snarled. 'You DON'T KNOW!' He struggled with his breathing. 'My God, but they ought to bring back mayflies and rose bowers and make you knight of the golden thistle or something.'

'You must keep calm,' Muller told himself. 'Calm; mock-modest; mock-humble.' He laughed self-effacingly. 'I'm sure it's all very difficult.'

'It's damn simple as it happens!' snapped McAllister. 'We're in Block Y and we'd have no chance if we weren't. The barracks is at the rear and so is the transport. If we swipe a car and get away it will be a miracle. But supposing we do? What then?'

'I don't know,' Muller said wearily. 'When people run for it they just run. They hope to get away.'

'Hope!' said McAllister. 'Hope!'

'Neil,' Muller implored. 'Isn't it a miracle that we're here at all? That we're alive? That we're sane?'

Breathing noisily, McAllister thought it over. 'I dunno. I don't think so. We've taken a lot. Other people would have gone under certainly; but they could have broken us up, and quickly. Vile things they could have done – horrible.'

'Perhaps they were to come,' Muller suggested.

'They were to come all right – pretty quickly in your case. My office was a sort of meeting place of the lesser lights and they talked.'

Muller frowned into the darkness. 'What did you do in that office of yours, Neil?'

'Do?' McAllister said irritably. 'What do you think I did? I compiled the damn record sheets you collected from old Edkins. Surely I don't have to tell you that?'

Muller didn't answer, and McAllister made a noise. 'Sort of thing they specialize in – thought it very comical.'

'Edkins ...' said Muller, speaking with an effort, 'had an idea that I might have to be ... drained. And someone else – the Inspector probably – said something about a tapthy-something treatment. What's that?'

'What would you think?' McAllister threshed about convulsively. 'They tamper with the glands. Switch one or two organs about. The result is grotesque; a loathsome caricature of a human being. But such creatures can't feel – or not much. They have no great capacity for suffering. That's why they didn't do it to us.'

'They might now.'

'Now, yes – if they didn't kill us at the first crack.'

'But other people would have gone under you said. Why other people? Why not us?'

'Because' – McAllister groped in the dark and tousled Muller's thinning hair – 'we're individuals. Most people today are out of moulds. They're predictable. They have no real personality or will. We're individuals so we've something to fight with. You' – this time McAllister squeezed Muller's shoulder – 'are a classic, you daft old sod. You have almost every weakness but you have mental strength.'

Muller smiled. 'Good old Mac!'

'The strength of your individualism or whatever it is. What is it, Muller?'

'I don't know. But I feel happier.'

'Don't be. Don't be,' McAllister said grimly. 'Our chances are nil.'

'If we can reach the coast,' Muller almost groaned.

'I doubt it. We'll try. We'll certainly try. But there's no salvation there. Ruins and a poisoned sea and –'

'Mac!' Muller bawled. The effort of shouting made the back of his neck throb and a numbing, icy pain creep over his head. 'Mac,' he said quietly. 'All this talk is getting us nowhere.' He paused and took a breath. 'What we have to do is pass the time – a lot of time. It's best to rest quietly. The thing is to lie on your right side until you can stick it no longer. Then turn over to your left. Then back to your right. Sooner or later you'll sleep. Perhaps,' Muller said painfully, 'we'll sleep most of the day. I hope so.'

McAllister was silent for quite a time. Then he said coldly: 'Turn from the right side to the left. And the left to the right. Is that how you rolled off to sleep in the old days?'

It was idiotic saying anything, Muller told himself, particularly when McAllister seemed more of his old self. It was ungrateful, too; but he felt exhausted and McAllister was getting on his nerves.

'The sleep expert,' said McAllister. 'Just had eight hours and wants to get in another sixteen.'

Muller sighed. 'I'm sorry, Neil. It was just an idea.'

'An idea!'

'In any case we won't be able to talk *all* day. We'll drive each other crazy. And we'll be overheard.'

'Overheard! In our steel and concrete tomb?'

'I don't know. I don't know,' Muller said wearily.

'They've a device that picks up the human voice. But not through steel and concrete – synthetic though it may be.'

'That does surprise me.'

'Clever. Oh you're a clever bastard! You've cooked our goose very cleverly!'

'Mac,' said Muller. 'They might hear us in the passage.'

'When the guard comes on duty, yes. But it's nowhere near dawn. It can't be more than four a.m.'

Muller turned over. 'If it's four a.m. it's dawn. It's summer you know.'

'Summer!' said McAllister. 'Summer!' He brooded for a moment. 'Wrote the most awful damn poem once. Don't remember much of it. Da-di-da-di-da-di-dadi-dee. It is not summer and we are not free.'

'Good,' said Muller. 'That sounds very good.'

'It's lousy. Juvenile wish-wash. And I was free when I wrote it – very free.'

'I like it.'

'You would – you probably influenced it anyway. But,' said McAllister, 'I'm wrong in saying I was free. I wasn't – free of myself or free of this. It's the best time though to write about captivity – when one is free.'

'Could be.'

'What would you write, Muller – now, I mean – if you had lights and paper and whatnot?'

'Write?' Muller blinked and moved slightly.

'What would you write?'

'I don't know.'

'You couldn't write a thing – not a thing. Your vitality has gone, your life force, everything. You're a vacuum, an empty flask. They've succeeded, haven't they?'

Muller felt a tingling of emotion. He turned sharply and his head throbbed. 'No.'

'If they haven't with you they have with me. God! Feel these walls! Slimy. And the air in this shaft's lethal. Like a black fog.' McAllister spat violently. 'My God, but I wish I'd kept my mouth shut about the P.D.W.s.'

Muller stared. 'You do?'

'I do. I *do*. There's something just a bit noble about you, Muller, but I'm not noble. I'm human. I like a good bed and four meals a day. What the hell is an idea or opinion set against that?'

'We don't look at it like that do we?'

'Don't we? I do – now anyway. So perhaps they've succeeded with me too.'

'Talk,' said Muller. 'It's so much talk. You don't mean what you say.'

'Don't I by God! I haven't your integrity, as I've told you, Muller. After a few days in Arm T I'd had enough – I'd had enough and I'm not ashamed to admit it. I grovelled, I fell flat on my face, I offered to publicly embrace the new order, but they weren't interested.'

Muller stared into the blackness. At last he said: 'I wonder why?'

'I don't know. Sheer indifference perhaps. I'm only a teacher – and an obscure one at that – so I have little status. I don't matter very much. You on the other hand have some sort of name and you make people *feel*.'

'Feel?'

'God knows how but you do. People,' said McAllister, 'don't *feel*, they don't feel or believe in anything. God used to be useful in emotional crises and at funerals and whatnot, but there's no faith now – no faith or belief in anything. Hence the importance of people feeling at least an *attachment* to something – to the town, the Committee, the wisdom of the authorities.'

Muller laughed. 'The town!'

'Wapsaw!' declaimed McAllister. 'I love thee, dear old Wapsaw, woozy as thou art! Thy soul is rich and rarer than any maiden's –'

Muller groaned.

'You certainly took the micky out of it years ago didn't you, Jimmy? And there you are you see. In the old days you'd have cleared off to London, but –'

'Neil!' Muller said sharply.

'– there was no London –'

'The lift! The lift you fool!'

'Lift?' McAllister said stupidly. 'What do you mean – lift?'

'I felt it move.'

'You're crazy!'

Muller sat up, his heart pecking jerkily. 'I tell you I felt it move.'

'Nonsense. It's your nerves, man. I've been afraid of –'

'How did you work the lift? What did you do to it?'

'Impelled it you fool. Electronically. Lifts nowadays are thrust –' This time there was no doubt. The lift dropped sharply for a few feet and the doors opened. The roof of the lift was two feet or so above the floor of the passage. Massive blue-uniformed men stepped forward but Muller could see little of them: the sudden glare of light blinded him. 'Out,' rasped a dreaded metallic voice.

Chapter 7

Jallen led the way: through many passages to a massive door and a large office. Muller's sight was still blurred, and his legs were trembling with shock and fatigue. He might have fallen, but two guards held him firmly.

Jallen sat down. His desk was fully ten feet long: bare except for a battery of instruments. Jallen dialled quickly and voices screeched at lightning speed. Jallen's finger jabbed and McAllister's voice crackled slowly into the room: 'They've a device that picks up the human voice. But not through steel and concrete. . . .'

Jallen switched off and sat back. 'First, cause. Immediate promotion to inspector. A brilliant bit of guesswork.'

'Fine piece of detective work, sir,' murmured one of his subordinates, and Jallen lit a cigarette.

'Same thing.' He scrutinized the prisoners. 'Give Muller a chair. If he doesn't sit down he'll drop.'

Jallen's senior officers were grouped each side of him as he blew out smoke venomously. 'Well,' he said. 'Well, well.'

He crushed the cigarette. 'After a thorough search and investigation we were satisfied that you hadn't left the building. We were also satisfied that you weren't in the building. In, that is, any normal place of concealment. We were baffled. But there were the bits and pieces stolen from your office McAllister. One of my men thought about them hard and long: the rest was inspired guesswork.'

Jallen sat back. His long fingers drummed the table. 'Technical knowledge and ability is useful nowadays. So is the will to kill. You killed two of my men, McAllister.

They were inefficient and deserved to die. But the jurisdiction wasn't yours. You are a murderer.'

The long eyes narrowed. The clipped voice was silent for a moment and the room was breathless.

'You might have been an asset to the town. Even to my force. You have ruthlessness and a certain amount of ability. And you have something that shows even now. Arrogance – physical superciliousness. I like that. It can be useful.'

McAllister in point of fact was – although erect – deathly pale, and Muller's tongue still seemed to be glued firmly to the roof of his mouth.

'In the lift shaft,' Jallen continued, 'you said – or inferred – that you would change your views if you were set free. Would you – if I found you a job on my staff?'

McAllister took a sharp breath.

'Would you?'

'Yes.'

'Why?'

'Because I'm sensible.'

'Is that all?'

'I don't want to die horribly.'

'Nothing else?'

McAllister hesitated. 'Yes. Nothing's worth what Muller and I have been through. Our ideas are wrong – we've been fools.'

'I see.' Jallen paused again and considered Muller. He considered him carefully and his brows tightened. 'Well, Muller, you look a sorry mess – a poor advertisement for almost anything human. I don't think a job on my staff would suit *you*. But supposing something could be found – or not found ... if we gave you a nice flat and a pension would you then conform and support the new order?'

Muller made a glugging sound.

'Well?'

'Not,' croaked Muller, 'without a change.'

'A change?' Jallen asked ironically. 'What sort of change?'

'Prisoners set free,' Muller said hoarsely. He took a breath.

'No more torture.'

'No more torture,' repeated Jallen. He seemed amused. 'And trial by jury. Would you like that?'

'I can't live with evil,' said Muller.

'Ah!' And Jallen slapped the desk with the flat of his hands and stared – almost accusingly – at his officers. 'It's the answer I expected. Now why can't the scientists explain this to me in a positive, scientific manner? Clinically. Chemically.'

'Perhaps he's mad, sir,' said a very large inspector, and Jallen stared at him even more distastefully than he had stared at Muller.

'He knows my offer is not genuine. And he's honest. Mad in his beliefs, but he is unlikely to change.'

'I think I could change him, sir,' said a pale superintendent, and Jallen again frowned distastefully.

'Of course you could. But torture isn't always logical. And look at him.'

They all stared at Muller, and Jallen said: 'Personally I am grateful to you. Inquiries have shown that you have no real backing. There's a bit of general dissatisfaction but that's to be expected. The authorities have nothing to worry about. You have, however, helped us to sort out the wheat from the chaff and that's all to the good. And now coffee – two pots.'

There was a flurry of movement and the coffee appeared very quickly.

'Give a pot to Muller. Pour it out.'

At the fourth attempt Muller lifted the cup to his lips. His hand was shaking badly and the hot liquid scalded his inside. Sweat sprang from his forehead but he drank a second cup quickly and felt better.

'Ah!' said Jallen. 'The inner man!' He wiped his lips. 'No Muller, don't give any to McAllister. You're to set out on a journey and you need the coffee. McAllister is to die very soon and it will be wasted on him.'

Another hush fell on the room. McAllister's pallor increased and Jallen breathed deeply and smiled.

'You tried to escape didn't you, Muller? You wanted to get away? You wanted freedom?'

The slashed face twisted. Muller swallowed hard two or three times – his tongue felt an inch thick – and said: 'McAllister shouldn't be singled out. It's only right that I should die with him.'

Jallen laughed. His aides – stiffly at attention – were a little uncertain, but Jallen glanced at them, and they shuffled quickly, and roared.

'Don't worry,' Jallen leered. 'You'll die. But artistically. Sportingly. In a fitting manner.'

He leant forward and slapped the table.

'You wanted freedom. I'll give it you. Unconditionally. What's more I'll give you a car. You can go anywhere you please. East, west, south or north. What do you say to that?'

Muller tried to look at McAllister, but McAllister was staring stiffly before him. 'I can't drive a car,' Muller mumbled.

Jallen's face was threatening, but it changed quickly to a look of sardonic amusement. 'Don't worry. There's nothing to it. A little button you press with your foot. Nothing else. Of course,' said Jallen, 'when I say you can go anywhere you can. But that doesn't include entering any town or resort. You have no papers and your description is known everywhere. As an added precaution you'll be watched from the air. But you'll be free. You don't like our town or society and we're not particularly fond of you, so I think I'm being singularly just and logical. There is, of course,' Jallen added genially, 'one other thing. Food and water. You'll need it in order to keep alive. But we can't help you there. You'll have nothing. No supplies at all.'

There was silence. One or two of Jallen's aides smirked, and McAllister said thickly: 'You bastard.' A guard hit him and he fell heavily to the floor.

'The logic of these rebels!' cried Jallen. 'The *logic*! They *wanted* to escape! They *wanted* to get away! They wanted freedom and starvation. They wanted what I'm giving them on a plate and they complain! What can you make of such people?' He sat back in the manner of an outraged man appealing for justice, and Muller – very quietly as McAllister rose shakily from the floor – said: 'I appreciate the – the irony of your decision. It's justifiable – your decision, I mean so far as I am concerned. But you speak of "them" and "they", as though I'm not to travel alone.'

Jallen's eyes gleamed. 'Ah,' he said softly. 'McAllister's a practical man. It's just possible – though unlikely – that he'd be able to do something. It wouldn't be sensible to release him. Neither is it sensible to release you, but you interest me.' The formidable face darkened, but the voice continued even more quietly. 'I knew little about you when you were detained. There were no special plans for you. You weren't important. You were inconvenienced a little – tortured if you like – and there was the possibility that you would die in some way. You didn't, but we're not particularly interested now in that type of endurance. It's a medical matter anyway.'

Jallen's face became even harder and his voice rose. 'The curious thing is why you should interest people and be able to withstand science.' He stared grimly, and McAllister – wiping blood from his mouth – laughed. 'The first answer is easy. In our splendid new society most people are content. They not only have to be, they *are*, and contented people make for happiness. But there are bound to be a few misfits – ambitious and frustrated, of course – and you attract them. It's inevitable. McAllister for instance would have found nothing wrong with the P.D.W.s if he'd been a headmaster.'

McAllister made a noise. 'I might have found something wrong with the slave workers down in the machine shop.'

'You wouldn't have known about them – and I doubt

if you would have wanted to know about them. Criminals. They're doing a useful job. But,' said Jallen, 'when I said science – that you, Muller, could withstand science – I should have said "logic". Science is another matter. If,' said Jallen, 'I take a two-hundred-years-old pistol and make it serviceable and kill you with it science has defeated you.'

'It takes two to make a war,' said McAllister. 'Suppose he had his own pistol and killed you? He would have defeated you, not science.'

Jallen – surprisingly – sat back and smiled. 'You're brave, aren't you, McAllister? And stupid – and an authority on pistols?' Slowly he lit another cigarette. 'I've killed a lot of men. Sometimes I enjoy it. Usually I'm indifferent. Occasionally reluctant. My interest in Muller's last days will be almost purely clinical, but I do get a kick now and then from killing, and I'll watch you go with quite a bit of satisfaction. It will,' said Jallen, 'be quite a tit-bit.' He blew out smoke. 'A pleasurable occasion – if on different lines to the bit of fun you had on your first visit to Block Y.'

McAllister reddened. 'First visit? What do you mean?'

'Strange thing, human nature, isn't it?' Jallen jeered. 'You show more perturbation than when you were knocked down just now. And not of course because you spent a few hours with a prostitute but because you were admitted to the building on a passcard taken from your deputy headmaster's pocket. You replaced the card before it was missed, but' – Jallen's lips twisted as he touched a button – 'you've been watched a long time, McAllister.'

*

'Throw that bleedin' cigarette away,' said a girl's voice – a light, attractive voice. 'I'm sick o' men who can't do without a smoke after they've 'ad it.'

The tape crackled as McAllister laughed. Muller blinked and glanced at the listening police officers. Most of them were frowning self-righteously.

'I don't blame you,' said McAllister. 'Awful stink. I wouldn't like to know what cigarettes are made of.'

''Ere's a kiss for not tellin' me,' said the girl. 'About ten times a day I 'ave to 'ear the bleedin' formula of somethin' or other.'

'Daft sods,' said McAllister. There was silence for a moment. Then he laughed and said: 'First time I've stroked a girl's bare belly.'

'You wouldn't be strokin' one now if it wasn't a slave day,' said the girl. There was a pause, then she said: 'First time? Do you like it?'

'Lovely,' said McAllister.

'Feels nice to me,' murmured the girl.

'Do you ever get hot about anybody?' asked McAllister. 'The real thing. Sort of love?'

The girl laughed. 'Sometimes.'

'It was a silly question. But you're a lovely girl.'

'Lovely!' she sniffed. 'I'm only a Grade II prostitute.'

'Grade II? Why only Grade II?'

'You know bleedin' well why,' the girl said fiercely. 'This is a man's world if you ain't an academical or got connexions. I was brought up in Block R an' I'm not fancy enough for the Grade I men. But they want prostitutes an' that's that.'

'Don't tell me you're not *satisfied* with life today?'

'Satisfied?' she hooted. 'That's a laugh if you like!'

'This is serious, you know, Janette – that's a lovely name by the way: Janette.'

'Well it was Janet really. You know – J-a-n-e-t.'

'Anyway I'm serious.' McAllister laughed and there was a sound such as a hand slapping bare flesh. 'Don't you know that you should be as happy as the day in this age of perfection?'

'Perfection!' said the girl.

'This is' – there was another laugh and a slap – 'an era of miracles. Of splendour. Of scientific wonders. Progress, my girl! Progress!'

'Progress!' she scoffed. There was a quick rustle of

movement. 'You can keep your bloody 'ands to yourself.' There was another rustle. 'Progress, balls! I'll tell you something,' she said. 'Science or no, men's pricks are the same as they was fifty years ago. Women 'ave to take 'em – 'ave the kids as well, an' there's nothin' bleedin' marvellous about that.'

'No,' said McAllister. 'Childbirth doesn't change much. They *can* make babies in laboratories I think but our overlords opted for the natural process. You're right when you say it's a man's world: they've taken advantage of the situation and re-asserted man's dominance. And *that*, baby, is the most reactionary thing of all.'

''Ere we go,' she said petulantly. 'I thought you was diff'rent but you're spoutin' away like all the other shaghole professors.'

'What's a shaghole professor?'

'They like to tell you all about your inside while they're inside you.'

'That's pretty filthy isn't it – though I must admit it shows a virility I lack. I wouldn't have the breath. No,' said McAllister, 'I'm nothing of that sort. I'm a rebel.'

'Rebel. What's a rebel?'

'I'm against authority – against our bosses. I'd like to overthrow them; by force if necessary.'

'God.' She sounded frightened. 'You want to be careful. If Jallen gets to know 'e'll 'ave your roe out.'

'Have you met Jallen?'

'Once.' She was afraid. 'Look – forget it. They listen in sometimes you know.'

'Don't be jittery, angel heart. I have an idea.'

'Forget it.'

'No, but look. The men you entertain. Your customers. Clients. They include police officers, don't they?'

'I'll say they do! My *God*!'

'Who are they – the coppers?'

'Inspectors to superintendents. Only chief supers an' over can go to the Grade I girls.'

'I'll bet they tell you a few things, don't they?'

'What're you gettin' at?'

'I just wondered – if they talk much.'

'*Talk!* My God, you should 'ear some of 'em!'

'Odd they're not overheard isn't it?'

'Don't be a dope!' she said witheringly. 'The coppers switch the bleedin' apparatus off before *they* talk!'

'Then can't you see how easy it is?' urged McAllister. 'Probably you don't like to offend such men. You put up with them – allowing the nasty, silent types to be silent and nasty and the talkative ones to talk.'

Janette laughed. Then there was a rumpled, smothering sound. And, for a moment, silence. She sighed before she spoke again. 'You're a funny old thing. An' you don't know tarts – or coppers.'

'I know coppers,' said McAllister.

'You don't. The biggest bastards can be the nicest – to us girls anyway.'

'It's difficult, I suppose, to be inhuman or dignified when one's pants are down.'

She laughed again. 'Don't you believe it! They can be starchy all right – an' nasty. They can do the wickedest things. Filthy. Broke many a girl up. But *talk*!' She laughed again. 'At times you'd think the town was bein' run from this room.'

'Maybe it is,' said McAllister. 'The town, I mean, run probably from rooms like this. But . . . is there one man who stands out . . . who talks more than the rest?'

'What're you *gettin'* at?' she asked.

'You'd like to be a Grade I girl wouldn't you? Think of it. Flash clothes and a maid and a flat in Block B.'

'I'd like a lot of things,' she said, 'but I don't want my guts ripped out. They're worked over enough as it is.'

'*Nothing* can happen to you,' urged McAllister. 'It's simple. Leave it all to me. Encourage one of them to talk until you hear something really hot. Tell me and I'll con –'

'Look mister,' she interrupted, a new hardness in her

voice. 'You've just met me an' you don't owe me a thing, but you're full of ideas. I don't know –'

'You bloody fool,' McAllister said angrily. 'I like you and I'd like to help you. But I don't like our despots one little bit and I'd enjoy putting one of them through it. That clear enough?'

'Mister,' said the girl, '*you* might enjoy it but I'd be dead. Blackmailin' a copper's a quick cremation.'

'Don't be idiotic,' snapped McAllister. 'Tyrants are usually cowards and the man would be scared stiff. I wouldn't reveal my identity naturally, but I'd make believe I was one of a group, and emphasize that other members of the group would nail him if I was traced or if anything happened to you.'

There was silence for a few seconds, then the girl sighed. 'It sounds fine. But take my advice an' forget it. You can't beat the coppers. If you knew what you were up against you'd –'

Jallen's finger jabbed and the recording ceased.

*

The silence was abrupt and dispelling. Muller – sitting rigidly – glanced quickly at McAllister, but McAllister didn't move for three or four seconds. When he did so the guards moved in.

'It's mad,' McAllister blustered. 'Crazy. Listening to a whore. A prostitute. A –'

'I was listening to you,' Jallen snapped, 'not the prostitute.' For a moment he glared, then he relaxed and sat back. His face twitched once, but he spoke very calmly and coldly: with metallic precision. 'The girl was sensible. Extremely sensible. In all the circumstances I shan't even downgrade her. If anything she's done us a service. So for that matter have you. But you're unreliable, untrustworthy and you can kill. On all accounts you're expendable.'

Almost before Jallen nodded the guards grabbed McAllister and marched him away. He tried to speak – and struggle – but couldn't, and Muller was still struggling with himself as Jallen spoke briefly to his aides, dismissing all but one of them.

Muller's heart was still thumping when Jallen sat back and considered him – this time with a mellow anticipation. 'And so another day starts, Muller. Time for a hot bath and breakfast. Time for the good people of Wapsaw to set about the day's business. Time for McAllister to die. Time for you to depart.'

Muller – a guard each side of him – sat awkwardly with an asphyxiating, paralysed feeling centred in his neck. It was difficult to breathe; difficult to see Jallen, although he was looking almost directly at him.

Jallen smiled. 'Time for a lot of things. Any comment?'

Muller still couldn't speak, and Jallen's fingers tapped lightly on his desk. 'I look what I am. Healthy. Normal. Authoritative. And you look what you are. Unhealthy. Abnormal. A broken man. You would do almost anything now wouldn't you?'

Muller made a blubbery, gurgling sound. The blood was pounding at his temples and something seemed to be choking him. At last he managed to swallow, and said hoarsely, 'No.'

Jallen's brows lifted questioningly – and mockingly. 'You wouldn't?' His fingers tapped rapidly. 'I think you would. If, for instance, I took you now to the mortuary where they lie – Searle of the Housing Department, Inspector Veale, Edkins and the rest: if I took you there and you saw the bodies, and McAllister standing at the end of the row . . . would you sign anything I put before you and broadcast in suitable terms to the people of Wapsaw . . . if it meant McAllister's life and yours?'

Muller swallowed twice. He nearly said no; he very nearly said yes; finally he mumbled: 'I might.'

Jallen laughed. 'You might. Of course you might. But no such mortuary exists. The corpses aren't corpses but fragments of dust. And nothing on this earth can save McAllister. Or you.'

For a moment he seemed to be enjoying a hidden source of amusement. Then he frowned. 'On the face of it *I'm* not being realistic. Physically you're a weakling and you have no reserves on which to draw. Without food and shelter you should die quickly and that would give little interest to my experiment. But' – he braced his chest – 'I come of a family of athletes, Muller. We've always had a great belief in the virtues of fresh air and water. That,' said Jallen, 'is what makes a man. Wind and water and good food . . . and the right ideas. You may' – his lips twisted – 'have some difficulty in finding a pool that's not contaminated, and you may not be the type – and for that matter may not have the strength – to enjoy a good bathe. But the fresh air will revive you.'

The guards smirked, and the young aide at Jallen's side bent his head in the best we-are-amused-but-don't-show-it-on-parade manner.

'There is,' Jallen repeated, 'nothing like fresh air – and nothing like fresh air plus hunger for creating an appetite. Satisfying the appetite is another matter. What you'll do I don't know. There's the coastal fringe with seaweed and so on and there's the sea itself. There have, however, been marine expeditions and some forms of life are recovering: have indeed recovered. How you'll trap and analyse any particular fish I don't know, but you were never much of a realist, were you, Muller?'

He rose – with immediate menace – to his feet, and Muller licked his lips. His head was throbbing; he put a hand to his temple and there was a red-hot twinge across his chest and a feeling of breathlessness.

'Any questions?' Jallen asked mockingly.

Muller was trembling slightly and he seemed to have no breath at all. His chest heaved; weakly and hoarsely he said: 'You can kill a man. His ideas will live.'

Jallen laughed. It was a slow laugh and it ceased abruptly. Leaning on the desk he said coldly, 'Not a very brave speech but brave enough in the circumstances. Courageous enough, but incorrect. You should have said:

"You can kill a man, but his ideas *can* live, or *may* live." "Can" or "may", Muller, not "will".'

The telephone rang and someone spoke briefly. 'Good,' said Jallen, and he replaced the earpiece, and sat down. 'When,' he said, 'you die you will vanish from the earth for ever. Not a particle of you will remain. Every word you have written has already been destroyed, and so has every man who has been attracted to your theories.'

There was a brief silence. Even the guards moved a little. 'McAllister's dead?' Muller asked hoarsely.

Jallen nodded. 'The last receptacle for your ideas. Dust already.'

Muller made an effort to clear his throat. Red-hot wires seemed to be percussing throughout his body. But he spoke a little more clearly. 'Until he killed the guards trying to escape McAllister had never harmed anybody.'

'No,' Jallen agreed evenly. 'But murderers have to start somewhere. There has to be a first killing.'

Muller avoided the obvious retort. There was no point in saying anything; and he was near the ultimate in exhaustion. He rubbed his eyes and took a laboured breath. 'These men I've influenced.... I don't know who they are. And my theories and ideas.... I'm not sure of those either ... at the moment.'

Jallen looked at him thoughtfully. 'No. Neither am I, even though you've just said that a man's ideas don't die with him. But you have had convictions or feelings that have impressed people or that people have accepted ... a sort of miraculous talent.'

Muller stared. 'Miraculous?'

'Certainly,' said Jallen. 'Here we have the remnants of humanity building and fighting for a new world. Life is so different from anything known in the past that we might just as well be on a strange planet. But no sane man alive today has asked for this – it's been forced on us *by* the past, by the political errors and human failings of the past, by the chicanery and scientific faults of the past. But you

...would return us to the past. Now that's one thing, Muller.'

'It's not a new thing,' Muller said huskily. 'Some of the men you've murdered used much the same argument.'

'I state,' said Jallen. 'Sometimes I announce. Often I proclaim. I don't argue.'

'Not even with the Committee?'

'Certainly not with the Committee. I,' said Jallen, '*am* the Committee.' The two guards and Muller stared and Jallen said incisively, 'I *am* the Committee, and I'm happy to tell you that the chance rocket that destroyed Canterbury and the Federal Government has made a City Congress necessary, and that it meets here in Wapsaw. I am reasonably confident that Wapsaw will be chosen as the new capital, and that Wapsaw will provide the nucleus of the new Government.'

The aide stood even more stiffly erect, and Jallen smiled grimly. 'What rhymes now, Muller? What derisive little jingles now?'

Muller cleared his throat violently. 'Hardly the time for it, is it? But things become clearer.'

'Not at all,' snapped Jallen. 'You have been under detention for some time and Canterbury was destroyed yesterday. There is no association. But –' he jumped up and strode to the window – 'the Canterbury incident strengthens my point about the realities – or facts, if you like – of the situation.' He stared out of the window. 'To you I'm evil. Ruthless and sadistic. Perhaps I am. But' – he turned back to his desk – 'recent history needs explaining only to a simpleton.'

Smoothly Jallen sat down. His chair – large and dark, like its occupant – was close to the desk, but Jallen moved into it without in any way touching it. He might have used suction. Somehow the feat made him more formidable, or sinister.

'There were more than forty-seven megadeaths and the first task was survival. Then renewal. It wasn't a question of wanting a new world, there was no choice. There had to be new towns with new methods of employment and residence. Above all there was no food. Food and its sources were hopelessly contaminated. There was famine and sickness. Before the artificial production of food was mastered a further two million people had died. Not,' said Jallen, 'a pretty situation. How would you have coped with it, Muller?' He stared grimly. 'How?'

Muller moved his eyes from the floor to Jallen's desk. 'Not by evil.'

'Or by good,' retorted Jallen. '*Or* by good,' he repeated – almost exultantly. He stared. 'Think, Muller. The niceties and inhibitions of thousands of years of civilization had gone. The survivors were saturated in evil. There was famine and radiation sickness. Large numbers of people were behaving like criminals. Now how would you have dealt with that? How?'

Muller didn't answer at once. 'I don't know.'

'You don't know. Wouldn't you have used sweetness and light? – the grace of heaven and your poetic spirit?'

'If you like.'

'If I like?'

'Yes,' Muller said wearily. 'Yes.'

'You would?'

'Yes. Yes,' Muller repeated. 'Yes!' he shrieked, losing all control. The blood hammered in his head and he trembled violently.

'That's better,' said Jallen. 'Much better,' he said the metallic rasp back in his voice. He sat back with satisfaction. 'Wouldn't have led to this, would it?'

Muller couldn't speak. He couldn't control his trembling and his heart was palpitating wildly.

'Would it?' said Jallen.

The guards each side of Muller lifted their hands threateningly, but the aide frowned.

'Would it?' Jallen repeated, and Muller dug the nails of each hand into the quicks of his fingers.

'Wouldn't have led to this, would it?' Jallen said again, and Muller took a shuddering breath.

'Would it?'

'No.'

'No?'

'No.'

'You're sure?'

With his head bent, Muller sat breathing heavily. The guards looked at him, then at the aide, who glanced at his chief.

'You're sure?' asked Jallen.

Muller lifted his head slowly. It seemed as if it wasn't there; as if he couldn't control it. He put his hand to it; the fingers to his cheek and the thumb beneath his jaw.

'You're sure?' Jallen asked again.

'No.'

'No?'

'Evil – no.'

'Evil?'

'Evil,' said Muller. He moved his hand. His voice was weak – more breath than sound. 'Evil – its continuance. Refinement.'

'Refinement?'

'You delight in its subtleties – in the refinements of evil.'

'I do?'

'In its continuance.'

'Ah,' said Jallen. Satisfied, he sat back. 'You have found a word, Muller. Now that,' he said emphatically, 'was the main task. The continuance of life and the establishment of law and order. Anarchy and disease had to be conquered and food had to be found. Food, Muller. Repeat the word.'

'Food,' breathed Muller. 'Food.'

'It grew everywhere – in the land and the sea and in the air. Then it didn't. It had to be made. So if you think, Muller, the survivors had to accept new ways of living and eating. That meant discipline: a severe control of most human emotions.' His eyes harshly condemnatory, Jallen leant forward slowly. 'You sought to release them: and you seemed to have a miraculous talent for doing so.'

Muller lifted a hand. It dropped again. 'Of all the non-sense! Of all the *nonsense*!'

'Nonsense?'

'I did nothing – nothing.'

'Nothing at all?'

'Years ago' – Muller fought for his breath – 'years ago. . . . I wrote a bit. That's all. Said what I thought.'

'Thought?'

'Yes.'

'You said what you thought about things?'

'Yes.'

'Did you have any thoughts about food?'

'Food!'

'It keeps us alive. You'll agree with that. I am of course,' said Jallen, 'speaking objectively. Food is artificially produced and for years very special precautions have been taken to safeguard it. Those precautions are unassailable. You must have known that. How, then, could you hope to succeed?'

Muller gestured agonizingly. 'To succeed in *what*?' His voice was shrill. 'I might have led a bunch of brigands or something. Can't you understand?' he shrieked. 'I was alone. *Alone*. I hoped to succeed in nothing. I didn't give a thought to food. Not a *thought*.'

'You *didn't*?'

'No. Except that it was vile. Awful. Used to taste like glue.'

'So it did. So it *did*,' said Jallen. He sat back. 'You think it tastes better now?'

Muller was trembling again: his heart seemed to be throbbing throughout his body.

'Personally,' said Jallen, 'I am obsessed with food. I love it. It interests me chemically and sensually. When scientists come to me with new ideas I often tell them to give me a formula for a really good Dover sole. You'll see my point, Muller. But,' said Jallen, 'my primary interest in food is professional. I have to guard it – against hostile action and insurrection. We might get precious little help from outside and if I failed Wapsaw wouldn't eat. Or it could eat if you like on the terms of whoever took over the manufacturing processes. You see the point?'

Muller tried to speak but could only gasp.

'Bend his head between his knees,' said Jallen.

One of the guards grabbed Muller by the back of the neck and forced his head between his legs. He tried to resist, but he was hopelessly feeble.

'Lift his head and do it again,' said Jallen. 'But this time hold his nose firmly.'

The guards got into a tangle, one of them holding Muller's head and the other trying to grip his nose. Quickly one of them dropped to his knees, putting his hand beneath Muller's legs to pinch his nose. Muller squirmed; the mists cleared, and he struggled painfully.

'Release him,' said Jallen.

Muller sat up, gasping and panting.

'Now answer my question. Do you see my point about food?'

Muller tried to answer, but couldn't.

'You see my point?'

The guards stood with hands poised.

'Do you see my point?'

The aide looked at Jallen.

'You see my point?'

'Yes.'

'But you gave no thought to food?'

'No.'

'You aroused passions. Breathed words of fire. But gave no thought to food?'

'No.'

'Not very *realistic* were you?' Jallen said harshly.

Slowly Muller looked at him. 'No.'

For the first time Jallen's face darkened. It became ugly and angry; vicious.

'I'll give you a taste of realism now. You prefer the

past: I'll give you a sample of it. The ruins, the suffering. Starvation and death.'

He stood up.

'Start him on his journey.'

Chapter 8

The magnostrat rose gently in a great arc to the west.

It was a wide road, pearly-grey, silvery in the sunlight and attractive compared with the dun-coloured concreted countryside. The two inside lanes carried the magnetized strip, a gleaming aluminium-like seam embedded in the road, but the outer lanes were orthodox, meant as they were for the use of cars with independent transmission, and the police Blips.

The ubiquitous Blips were little larger than a car, blue-black wasp-shaped things uncannily silent in approach but viciously noisy in passing. Very fast, they could take off and land within yards. After driving slowly for about an hour Muller stopped. Two or three times he had jumped as Blips passed overhead – they emitted a peculiarly piercing shriek – but they hadn't approached him, and not once had he seen another car. It was Tuesday or Wednesday – Muller couldn't remember which – not the time when people travelled to and from the health resort, but the emptiness and isolation against the lunar-like ghostliness of the countryside would in more normal circumstances have been unnerving. Now Muller felt almost comforted.

He had travelled at no more than 5 m.p.h. and he stopped and looked back at Wapsaw. It was strangely beautiful. The ground for five miles around towns had been saucered-out, and the milky clouds floated above the white towers of Wapsaw like symbols of purity guarding silvered shrines. It was like a vision of a celestial city, so lovely that tears came to Muller's eyes, and so false that the tears dried. Grimly he stared, but the sternness gradually left his ravaged face, to be replaced by a look of sadness, then, almost, of death.

Slowly, tiredly, Muller rubbed his eyes. It was warm in the car, beautifully warm, and comfortable, beautifully, beautifully comfortable. He closed his eyes, and slept.

*

'Blip S.O.23 No. 2049 Sgt. J. O. Johnson reporting, sir. We are alongside the car. The man Muller appears to be asleep.'

'What do you mean "appears"?'

'He is asleep, sir.'

'Then let him sleep. He has plenty of time.'

*

They had marched him across the vast square, past the marching recruits and rows of cars. Drill sergeants barked and Blips shrieked overhead. A car was waiting and Jallen's aide spoke to the inspector in charge of the I.T. unit. Muller was held – practically supported – by the guards, and the inspector looked worried. He talked earnestly, but the aide shook his head stiffly. A group of sergeants and drivers stared at Muller as the inspector said, 'But can't you ask Mr Jallen, sir?' The aide turned abruptly. 'Mr Jallen's gone to bed. You have your orders.'

The inspector – red-faced and grim – stared after him, then snapped: 'All right. Put him in the car.' Muller was pushed into the driver's seat, and a sergeant – '*Not* with the engine on,' barked the inspector – explained the controls. There was little to explain. Left button to start; right button to stop. 'That's all,' said the sergeant. Left button for the engine; right button for the brakes. 'That's *all*,' said the sergeant. 'To make the car go you depress the left button. Press it with your foot. Press the left button with your left foot. *But don't press hard.*' At last Muller was told to have a go. He tried to take the steering wheel but it seemed immense and far away. His arms shook and sweat trickled down his forehead. The sergeant looked at the inspector and the inspector stamped angrily away. Five or six times he marched up and down before turning back to the car.

'He'll kill somebody, sir,' the sergeant began. 'A man half-dead in charge of a –' but the inspector jumped into the rear seat and told the sergeant to take the wheel. 'Get him out of the town. That's all we can do. Order one-and-one.' The car moved off quickly, and the sergeant barked into the telephone.

The drive through Wapsaw stirred Muller, but only slightly. It took less than three or four minutes to clear the town, and the familiar sights and scenes passed all too quickly. After the last two or three weeks they seemed oddly unfamiliar; like fragments of a dream vaguely remembered. Muller knew he was seeing Wapsaw for the last time, but he was too exhausted, too stunned emotionally to feel anything except a mild anger. McAllister was dead; for many years they had walked these streets, not always happy but free.

Five miles out of the town the car stopped. The attendant car waited and a Blip circled overhead as the inspector and sergeant looked at Muller. 'Suppose he –' the sergeant said softly, ramming one hand into the other. 'Wouldn't it be best if the Blip was to. . . .' and the sergeant pressed an imaginary trigger, but the inspector shook his head. 'He's to be left alone. A-lone. Chief's orders.' He stared at Muller. 'You understand that? We're leaving you now. You can drive on. Leave the road before you reach R3. Understand?' There was silence for a moment, then the inspector stared out of the car window, and – very loudly – said: 'Personally I'd have a SLEEP. I'd have a LITTLE SLEEP. I'd drive VERY SLOWLY for a few miles then stop and REST. There are no orders against it so I'd REST.'

After they had left him Muller sat quite still. For the first few minutes he was without emotion. Then a spasm of fear gripped him; glancing over his shoulder he grabbed the steering wheel jerkily and stabbed the accelerator button. The car roared wildly across the road and Muller spun the steering wheel. He completely forgot the left-button-right-button business and his foot remained on the power pedal; but it slipped from it as the car vibrated violently. It snaked away from the magnetized strip and rolled slowly towards the outer traffic lane. Muller's heart was bumping again and he was shaking badly.

He sat still for a few minutes, then – very softly and gingerly – touched the power button and straightened the car. He removed his foot from the button and the car stopped. Three or four times he repeated the process. When the button was pressed very gently and then released the car moved extremely slowly and stopped almost at once. Muller pressed the button a little more firmly; this time the car travelled for about twenty yards, hesitated for a moment, then – as though remembering something – started to roll backwards. It was three or four seconds before Muller remembered the brake button. 'Fool,' he muttered.

Slowly he moved forward again. His mind was hazy and curiously blank. The facts he had to face – starvation and death – seemed quite nebulous. Everything for that matter had a feeling of unreality. McAllister was dead and nothing else mattered. A lump came into Muller's throat and his hands tightened on the huge steering wheel. His aching eyes moistened and the road for a moment was a blur. But if Muller had any predominant emotion it was puzzlement. He couldn't – at the moment at least – feel deeply, and his brow had a furrow of bewilderment. Death had always upset him. When anyone he had known well had died he had been upset for days, but now there was little feeling in him.

Slowly the car rolled towards the sea. The sun was shining quite brightly but Muller felt cold. Must be a heater, he thought. He touched a button, and nothing happened; a second button, and nothing happened; a third button, and something did. Soon he was warm; but the warmth increased his muzziness and fatigue and made his genitals – which were still swollen and sore – throb painfully. 'Poor old Kitty One-Eye,' thought Muller. He wondered what she would do in a situation like this. One thing was certain; she wouldn't go meekly to her death.

Slowly – very slowly and painfully – Muller tried to think about it. First, there was acquiescence. One had to accept the fact of death. But few people, in the present situation, would doubt the inevitability of death. And to avoid further suffering they would take refuge in death. With a car it was easy. But there were two points. Jallen was accustomed to dealing with an almost totally complaisant population. There was no political opposition and very little crime; nothing, in fact, to oppose his will. There was, of course, no army or navy now, and no air force as such, but Jallen had certain responsibilities for defence, duties that were no longer onerous. He had time to think. 'And has he,' thought Muller, 'analysed me only too well?'

Jallen's submissive subjects and absolute authority wouldn't diminish his confidence and faith in his own judgement. But there were two forms of submission, the mental and the physical. Totally submissive people were, of course, mentally *and* physically submissive, but it was the physical side that stood out. It was the most apparent, the most obvious. When one judged a man one looked at his physique, at his face and body. And what was easier than picking out a broken man?

'Poor old Neil' – thought Muller as the car crawled westwards – 'was certainly the sort of man Jallen would fear.' Fear, perhaps, was too strong a word, and McAllister certainly had had many qualities of heart and mind, but his dominance was physical. He had a positive personality, he asserted or declared himself physically; he had not been without a certain amount of deviousness, but the man and his intentions couldn't be mistaken. Imprisonment and torture had diminished him, but not broken him.

McAllister had always been assured, frank and fearless and *definite*, and the picture at the end wasn't totally obscured. He hadn't been *meek*; Jallen wouldn't have given him a car.

The road was no more than a blur and Muller stopped. He swallowed painfully. Even now he could hardly accept it, the facts of the last few weeks and the fact of McAllister's death. Perhaps he *wasn't* dead, perhaps he would pop up somehow. Perhaps he would; it would be just like him. 'But I'm being childish,' Muller told himself, 'and my thinking is woolly. Hopelessly woolly. I'm thinking,' Muller told himself, 'in terms of a physical man, a man of action; but wasn't it simply a question of *character*? It would be to Jallen. Men like Jallen were usually impressive physically, and they tended to judge a man by his appearance, by his outer shell. Jallen might well be (and probably was) an exception, but he has assessed me,' thought Muller, 'as a coward, a weakling who will do nothing startling or courageous physically; an introvert who will submit meekly to starvation and death.'

Muller rubbed his eyes and pressed the button. He was breathing heavily and the concreted countryside heaved before him like banks of fog. 'Must rest,' he told himself; 'must rest. I'm not dead yet,' he told himself, 'but I feel dead; much like a man near to death must feel.' There was a choking, compressive feeling around his heart, and Muller wondered if it were damaged. It might be; Muller pressed his hand to it and the breathlessness increased. 'Dope,' he muttered; 'probably the dope.' He drove on muzzily. The road came at him, sort of sucked into him, but he kept his foot on the button. 'There was one thing,' he told himself; 'the sea.' He would see it and hear it. The countryside symbolized modern life, it was sprayed from the air with a chemical that set the soil like rock, but the sea – poisoned though it might be – would look the same and feel the same. There would be the same music, the wind and the waves and the feeling of freedom. Jallen at least had given him that. Ironically, perhaps, but there were worse places to die. 'I'll see the sea,' Muller told himself, 'but I'll stop now and rest. Have a last look at Wapsaw. See Wapsaw and . . . what?'

*

When he awoke a woman was staring at him.

'Are you all right?' she asked.

Muller could only mumble.

'Are you ill?' she said.

'I,' Muller said thickly. 'I . . .' and she stared at him, not exactly with horror, but with intense curiosity.

'We passed you some hours ago on the way to R3 to fetch a relative. You were slumped over the wheel, just as you were now. We're on our way back, and. . . .'

Her voice tailed off, and Muller sat up. There was a car across the road with a man and a woman staring at him.

'I . . . I . . . I'm Muller. Name's Muller. Been under arrest.'

She stared – not with surprise. 'Under arrest?'

'I . . .' he retched and coughed violently. 'I . . . had to be rehoused. House had to come down. They questioned me. I'd done nothing, but. . . .'

'Beautifully typical.' She was about fifty, pale and hard-faced, and she stared intensely. '*House*, you say. You must be Muller the writer. James Muller.'

Muller nodded, and started coughing again. 'I remember your books. They were good. But' – she stared – 'have you sort of escaped?'

'No.' He rubbed his eyes. 'I've been in Block Y. They've released me but . . . I can't enter any town or anything.'

The woman's mouth hardened. Her husband called from across the road and blared the car's horn. The woman still stared, and her husband – elderly and nervous – appeared at her elbow.

'What *is* it, Irma?'

She moved a little and motioned.

'Good God!'

The man flinched and turned away quickly.

'This poor devil,' his wife said grimly, 'has been cast into the wilderness to starve and die.'

Her husband shuffled uneasily. 'Yes, yes, but –'

'But nothing,' snapped his wife. 'This man is or was James Muller the novelist. A fine writer and utterly harmless. We should help him.'

'Help him! But –'

'In the name of what was human decency we ought to help him. Couldn't we hide him in the flat?'

'The flat!' He stared. 'Are you *mad*?'

'I don't think so.'

'But, but' – he glanced upwards – 'I doubt if we could get him *into* the flat. We couldn't without being seen. And if we could he couldn't stay there for ever. Without papers he –'

'You men are all cowards,' she said harshly. 'Every man jack of you. No wonder things like this happen.'

'Irma,' her husband said desperately, again glancing at the sky. 'If they see us. If –'

'Don't be idiotic,' she snapped. 'We're simply looking at a stranger we think is ill. Who *is* ill. We can't leave him to starve and die. Not this stranger.'

Her husband looked at Muller and his eyes flickered. 'I doubt if he has far to go. But think, Irma. It wouldn't come off. There would be the fullest investigation when they found the car empty. Within an hour or –'

'Wait a minute,' she said. She stared hard at Muller. 'Do you know Rhyl – R3?'

Muller shook his head.

'The old place went of course. R3 is made up of the camp and two apartment blocks. Little else. This road takes you into R3 and straight to the camp gates. They're always open. On the right of the gates is the office. Now' – she considered Muller – 'it's a thousand-to-one chance I know but your position is hopeless anyway.'

'Irma,' said her husband beseechingly, staring at the sky.

'Irma's foot. Now listen, Muller. In the hut next to

Gelda – my sister – was a man not unlike you. I saw him. He's thin and elderly and he's sure to die. He's had a bad seizure and they were carting him –'

She stopped as Gelda violently blared the car's horn. For a moment she hesitated; then she ran across to the car.

Her husband stared again at the sky and wiped his brow. He glanced at Muller, fumbled in a pocket, and – guiltily and furtively – produced a flask. 'Sorry I didn't think of it before,' he said.

Muller's hand was unsteady. He drank quickly and deeply and for a second or so felt nothing; then liquid fire spurted from his genitals to his throat and his head slammed savagely. Choking and spluttering, he heaved and was sick; then – holding his head – he bent over the wheel in a paroxysm of coughing.

The woman came back and glanced at him. 'You *bloody* fool,' she snapped at her husband. She withered him with a look, then turned again to Muller. 'Never mind. It may help to clear your system.' She waited as Muller (hands badly shaking) dabbed his streaming eyes. 'Now wipe up that muck with your jacket and PULL yourself together.'

Again the car's horn blared and a Blip shrieked in the distance. 'Now listen Muller,' she said urgently. 'Things like this are just not done and never have been done so that gives you a chance. Listen,' she said. 'The man's name is Sims and the chalet number is 89. They've taken him to hospital but his papers and things may still be in the hut. You need identification papers with a photograph and a travelling permit. Perhaps you can alter them or something. It's a wild chance but your only one.'

Again a Blip shrieked and again Gelda blared the car's horn.

'I'm off, Muller. Here's my husband's razor and a packet of food. Eat and shave first. And here' – she tugged violently – 'is my husband's jacket. It'll fit at a pinch.'

Her husband stood shaking and her hands flew over the

jacket pockets. She handed the jacket to Muller and looked at the sky.

'They didn't see us but they'll soon be back. Good-bye Muller. And for what it's worth . . . God bless you. . . .'

*

The outer gates were wide open, and so were the inner gates. Muller stopped the car out of sight of the office, and walked through the gates. Every second he expected to be called back, but the woman in the office had her head bent, reading something, and a fearsome noise was coming from a large building on the left, obviously the dining hall.

Muller walked cautiously and curiously stiffly, like a sick man just out of bed, or a drunkard trying to follow a white line. The tension of the last hour had been considerable, and he jumped alarmingly as loudspeakers blasted the air with. 'Tonight-tonight-tonight at EIGHT a free concert for ALL by Roy Roxy's R3 Revellers! Wackity whack-whack whack whack-whack Ho!' Music crashed, and Muller walked on, sweating profusely.

The concrete drive was wide and long, straight for a hundred yards or so, then it forked. Muller took the left fork, and crossed a small concrete bridge. There was a stream beneath it dyed a brilliant blue: Muller blinked, and walked stiffly up a narrow path bordered on each side by strips of artificial grass and small concrete chalets, dazzlingly coloured. Rubbing his eyes, Muller reached a large white building labelled 'REGENERATIVE BATHS: CHILDREN KEEP OUT', but the path continued to the left, and everything seemed quieter. There was a last row of chalets, bluish in colour, and a fence some twenty feet high, off-white and metallic.

Chalet number eighty-eight – lately occupied by Gelda – was near the end of the row, on the right, and Muller's objective, close to the boundary fence, was shadowed discreetly by the waning sun. Muller didn't hesitate: Irma's husband's grey jacket fitted badly and contrasted oddly with the remedial extension trousers. 'Should've carried the jacket over your arm, you idiot,' muttered Muller (the startling trousers might easily have been taken for beach garb); but he didn't make the mistake of trying the door. It was bound to be locked, but the window was wide open and less than two feet from the ground. He tumbled through, striking a chair. For some minutes he lay dazed on the chalet floor, breathing heavily. His mouth was dry but he was saturated in sweat, and his heart was pounding away savagely.

It was a one-roomed chalet. There was little furniture: bed, table, two chairs, recessed wardrobe. Muller sat up and looked about him, then he dragged himself to his feet and made for the bathroom. It lacked a bath (the room for that matter couldn't have measured five feet by four) but there was a wash basin. Muller swilled out his mouth and drank glass after glass of water. After the fifth or sixth glass he paused, leaning over the basin with both hands on it. After a moment or so he looked up, and glanced in the mirror above the basin. He froze, and his heart tremored icily. For a moment his mind didn't function: all he knew was that the game was up and someone was staring at him. Then, as he began to realize that he was in a tiny room staring into a small mirror, a mirror dimensionally incapable of reflecting more than one face, a face that was his, he felt a sense of disbelief.

The hair had receded badly and was very thin. The eyes were about half their former size and were deeply sunken. The skin around them was white and gummy, and the eyelids hung heavily. The nose, formerly small, now seemed larger, and was purplish-veined near the bridge. The cheekbones now seemed high and they were fiercely red, in sharp contrast to the greyish-white of the shrunken face. The cheeks were hollow, and skin was flaking from the grooved lips. But the temples upset Muller more than anything else. They had fallen in so badly that a small egg could have been placed in the cavities, and the temporal arteries were cruelly exposed.

Profoundly shocked, Muller turned slowly, and walked to the bed. He sat down heavily and tried to think. It was difficult to think and not easy to feel. He wasn't indignant. If anything he was puzzled. Life was evil, and it took some understanding. 'I am not,' Muller told himself, 'being realistic, not being realistic, as Jallen would say, but anyone, surely, should be satisfied? Even Jallen, seeing a face like that, should be content?'

Muller sat for a long time, trying to think about it. It was a final illustration (if one was needed) of the totality of evil. But to follow any such line of thought implied acceptability, an acceptance of death, and he hadn't accepted death. It wouldn't be a difficult matter to sever those protruding arteries. 'Perhaps,' thought Muller, 'it's simple. They're nearly all such strapping big fellows nowadays, and they wouldn't be able to understand how a weakling could go through the mill and survive.' Jallen may have said something of the sort (he couldn't remember what Jallen had said) but perverted people had always derived some sort of satisfaction from seeing a helpless animal die, particularly if the animal was wounded or peculiarly diseased. Animals, of course, were a thing of the past, but there were human animals.

Muller took a sharp breath. There was no point in being afraid: there was no longer any point in being afraid. 'They can't hurt me any more,' he told himself, 'they can't torture me any more, not with a face like that.' Slowly he got up and walked back to the mirror. Carefully he inspected his face. It took a certain nerve. The skin, of course, was easily explained; confinement and inadequate nourishment had impaired it. 'The face,' Muller told himself (*the* face, not *my* face), 'had for that matter always been thin and ascetic; a face that had quickly wilted under stress and strain. The nose, of course, the *nose* was bound to look larger now that the face was smaller (did noses shrink?) and the eyes hadn't been unlike this after illness and so on.'

Muller blinked. Come to think of it they had been larger

and not smaller, particularly after nervous strain. They had seemed immense. He could still remember his mother scolding him when – in his teens and twenties – he had returned home late after hours of argument. His eyes, normally large and lustrous, had been quite immense then, with a strained, staring look. 'You've been at it again,' his mother would say. 'You've been at it again.' But his eyes had long since lost the size and colour of youth, and they *had* seemed to diminish further during serious illness. Even the temples – never *round* of course, or fleshy – had subsided just a *bit* in recent years, and they had seemed to cave in a little more after acute strain. Afterwards they filled out again, leaving reddish sort of marks from the veins or arteries or something.

'Hair's certainly receded,' thought Muller. 'Receded two inches or more in three weeks; fluffyish and grey at the sides and very thin and greying on the top. Never thought I'd go bald: always had a good head of hair and there was no baldness in the family.' Muller stared grimly – and nearly laughed. 'Trying to explain things, aren't I,' he told himself; 'trying to explain or compromise; no, not explain or compromise; accept.'

Slowly he walked to the wardrobe and inspected it. There were two suits, a green-and-yellow check, and a brown. Muller tried on the brown jacket. It fitted quite well; remarkably well. Mr – what was his name? – must have been thin; *extremely* thin. Muller ran a hand through the pockets: empty. He tried the check suit. No wallet, no anything; not even a New England cent. 'Obviously,' thought Muller; 'they wouldn't leave the man's papers and money lying around.' There was no bureau in the room, no cupboard or place of concealment. Muller thought for a moment. Both the suits looked new and freshly pressed; they didn't seem to have been worn much, or to have been worn recently. Muller walked to the head of the bed and glanced behind it. Yes; a pair of grey trousers, roughly folded, lay on the floor. Again Muller glanced round the room. Now where was the jacket? 'Fool,' he muttered. On the near side of the door was a partition about six feet long, fitted probably to keep out draughts or to give some impression of privacy. There was a coat hanger on the other side of the partition. On the hanger was a rather grubby grey jacket. The papers were in the breast pocket.

Muller looked at them. They belonged to Alan Robert Sims of 197 Block O, Wapsaw. 'Sims,' Muller muttered. He removed the jacket and washed his face and hands. It took an effort. 'Sims,' he muttered. Mr Sims according to his photograph wasn't much like Muller, but he was thin and elderly, balding, with a tight, strained look. It would do. 'I'm not old,' thought Muller, 'but I look it. I've been ill. So has Sims. He's ill now, or dead. Sims – now where did he keep his shirts? – has been ill. Sims, Simson. Of course. SimsON. Easy. Too easy.' Muller picked up a suitcase and walked out. The campers would soon be returning from tea and he needed a typewriter.

The suitcase was empty but Muller still walked slowly with the chained-leg feeling. There were concrete paths all over the place: he walked up four or five, passing chalet after chalet, before he saw one with a typewriter in the window. He walked straight in and changed Sims to Simson. The type size was about the same but the 'ON' looked fresher and the colouring was a bit different. 'Nothing I can do about it,' thought Muller; 'just have to chance it.' He changed the address to 2197 Block O – hitting the keys heavily – and made for the office.

He was sweating again, and tension clawed him, but he walked on steadily. 'Point is,' he thought, 'I *look* harmless, look like a sick and tired old man; but there were the technicalities. The technicalities. McAllister would have been the man for this. Taken it in his stride.' Muller walked on steadily, steadily but slowly, keeping to the left side of the drive so that he would be out of sight of the office for as long as possible. But the woman was still reading – some sectic rubbish undoubtedly – and he was in the outer office, standing at the counter, before she saw him.

'I've come,' said Muller.

The woman gaped.

Muller's heart was tattooing and his voice was weak and hoarse. He tried to clear his throat. 'I've arrived,' he said.

The woman stared, her mouth open a little. She was rather unpleasant-looking, thin and pallid. 'Looks as if she could do with a holiday at R3,' thought Muller. She stared, and said: 'You've *what*?'

'I've arrived,' said Muller. 'Happy holidays!' He tried to laugh, and made a ghastly, ghoulish sound. The woman moved away a little, and Muller – with as much severity as he could manage – said: 'Have you had the message?'

The woman's sectic strip fell to the floor. She paled and said, 'Message?'

Muller pursed his lips. 'See this goes no further. Understand?'

'I think I'd better get –' said the woman, her finger straying towards a button, but Muller slapped his papers on the counter with a startling gesture originated by a nervous spasm, and, in a voice that emerged as a rasping croak, said: 'It's the Office. Understand?'

The woman paled further and her jaw dropped fully an inch. 'Office?'

'Office of Statistics,' said Muller. 'We've had complaints. But keep this to yourself.'

His legs were wobbling and his frightening glare was due mainly to the difficulty he had in focusing, but the woman licked her lips. 'I won't tell a soul.'

'I'm the Chief Inspector,' said Muller. 'Retired, of course. See the idea?'

'Oh yes, sir!' the woman said fervently. 'Of course, sir!'

Muller leant on the counter: he had to. 'We're not fools, you know. This has been going on a long time.'

'Oh sir, I know! They've all been at it! But I've done nothing. My conscience is clear!'

'We know. So keep this to yourself.' Muller's voice,

meant to be soft and conspiratorial, was a harsh crackle. 'Where's the Director? Tell me that.'

'In bed with the 'flu.' The woman sniffed. 'At least that's what *he* says!'

'Book me in,' rasped Muller. 'Incognito of course. Elderly holiday-maker.' His head bobbed startlingly as his knees knocked. 'Flu, eh? In 1999?'

'Oh sir!' said the woman. 'The goings-on! Drink and women and –'

'My car's outside. See it isn't moved.' Muller gripped the counter with both hands. 'Now give me my papers.'

With great alacrity the woman scribbled on five cards, and stamped them. 'Here's your chalet card sir. Number eighty-eight. Here's your dining hall permit and your beach permit and –'

The loudspeakers roared and a Blip shrieked past as two huge blondes – stark naked – strolled down the drive.

'. . . it's an entitlement to a Blue holiday only but there's nothing else available unless you'd like us to turn out a Red or a White. For your purposes sir, I do think. . . .'

Slowly Muller walked down the concrete drive. People were about now, elderly couples and children mostly. They stared, and a nude green-haired girl crossing the bridge smiled invitingly.

Muller was trembling as he unlocked the door of Chalet number eighty-eight. He dropped the case to the floor, removed his jacket, and hit the bed. 'Irma,' he muttered, and slept.

*

'Wakity-wakity shakity-shakity loosen your leg and S-H-A-K-E it!' roared the loudspeakers, and there was a blast of trumpets that made Muller jump as he stood outside the dining-hall entrance.

A large red-faced man in a startling red uniform approached him.

'Are you a Red or a Blue?'

'Blue.'

'Then get in the Blue queue!'

Muller had risen early in the hope of avoiding the worst of the crowds and noise, but he was not alone: the huge dining hall already held two or three hundred campers. Muller stood stiffly and sat awkwardly, and although hundreds of tables were empty the Blue marshal led him to a table that seemed crowded. Its occupants – a family probably, of father, mother and son – were very fat and very red, but with curiously expressionless eyes like dirty old glass. The family had already fed, or were waiting for a second breakfast: six eyes stared unwaveringly (but with an unnervingly sightless effect) at Muller: he swallowed a cup of tea, gulped a mouthful of food and left. He was sweating again and he gulped the cool morning air. 'Arm T was almost preferable,' he muttered.

He turned to the left, circuiting the enormous building. To the left of the dining hall was the Hall of Joy, then a gate and the beginning of the boundary fence. Walking slowly (he felt tireder than the previous evening) Muller passed through the gate, and found himself on the car park. It was about two hundred yards by fifty, bordered by the outer (mesh) fence and the road, with the entrance gates in the distance.

Keeping close to the wall, Muller slowly walked the length of the building. Not a soul was in sight, and the three parked cars – one of them his – looked oddly lonely but he was acutely apprehensive. It was this or nothing.

After a long, oblivious sleep he had spent four hours of tortured conjecture, from which he had emerged with little except doubt. It was all so pat, the Irma episode and the failure of the Blips to observe his entrance into R3, the illness of Sims and the officewoman's acceptance of him. It smelled; 'Just the sort of little game Jallen might like to play, but is it,' Muller had asked himself, 'is it *them*, and is it *me*?' The whole thing might have been contrived, but acting was practically a defunct profession, and Irma and her husband, if they were acting, were exceptional actors. Muller could believe that they were, if only for the reason that no one in Jallen's world would dream of taking the risk they had taken. And yet Irma herself was credible and possible somehow, and Muller could scarcely believe that the officewoman had been acting. It was the same with Sims' papers; it was possible (though difficult) to believe that they had been left lying around, but how were they to know that he (a sick and *un*practical man) would be capable of finding a typewriter and altering them? 'It was all very dubious, but' – Muller thought – 'somehow just possible': what worried him most was the apparent failure of the Blips to spot him entering R3. It was true that he had driven very slowly for sixty miles and very quickly for thirty. And it was true that the first stage of the journey had been punctuated by a long sleep; the first stage, therefore, had taken nine or ten hours, and the second stage ten or twelve minutes. The Blips (unless they had special orders to do so) may have wearied of watching him; they may for that matter have been watching the nude beauties of R3.

Slowly Muller walked towards the parked cars, his left hand touching the blank wall of the Hall of Joy. As he neared the rear of the dining hall he could hear kitchen noises, and there were staff entrances and windows. Without pausing Muller pocketed a key carelessly left in a door: near the next door was a rod affair used presumably for clearing drains: he hesitated, cracked what he hoped was a storeroom window, and hurried away as quickly as he could. As he turned into the drive an imposing individual in a blue uniform stopped him.

'And where do you think *you're* going?' he said.

Muller was sweating and his heart was pounding: he made a glugging noise.

'I *said* where do you think *you're* going?' snapped the marshal. (He must have been the Chief Blue marshal judging by his uniform.)

'I'm out of condition,' gasped Muller.

'You look as if you're out of the boneyard,' the marshal retorted.

'I know,' said Muller. 'I thought I'd have a quiet snooze somewhere.'

The marshal stared. 'You *what*?'

'Thought I'd relax for a few hours.'

'You did, did you? Has it,' the marshal said severely, 'occurred to you that you're on holiday?'

'That's the idea,' said Muller.

'It may be *your* idea, but the idea *here* my friend is recreation.'

'Oh I know.'

'I am,' the marshal said coldly, 'referring to re-creation and not wreck-creation. That's our job, my friend. To renew, revitalize and re-establish the human system. And that means a programme.'

'Quite,' said Muller.

'*You* will take a bit of revitalizing but *I* will take a personal interest in the matter. Now where's your programme?'

'I haven't got one yet. I was thinking more about the girls.'

The marshal stared. 'You *what*?'

'The nudes one sees strolling about. They're the camp prostitutes presumably.'

The marshal took a slow uneven breath. 'Our *hostesses*, my friend, are the cream of New England. They are not referred to as *prostitutes*. And they are not meant for dirty old men like you.'

'Quite,' said Muller. 'I'm not without money of course.'

The marshal gazed aloofly at a high cloud. 'Money?'

'I haven't had time to spend any have I?'

'H'm. I suppose not.' The marshal unbent. 'So you'd like a girl, eh?'

'Well,' said Muller, 'there are probably worse ways of passing the time.'

The marshal chuckled and tickled Muller under the testicles. 'Dirty old dog aren't you?'

'You know how it is,' said Muller.

Again the marshal chuckled. 'It's early in the day of

course – bit *early*, eh? – but I may be able to find a girl who wasn't on duty last night.'

'Try to find a pacific type,' said Muller. 'You know: interesting but restful.'

The marshal gazed down at him quizzically. '*Restful*? I doubt if any of our girls are that.'

Muller had been standing with intense rigidity; and a combination of acute tension and the exhaustion that no amount of sleep seemed to throw off was almost too much. He slipped, as though he had been kicked, and his face twitched with a nervous spasm.

'Been overdoing it, eh?' said the marshal. 'Not as young and fit as we were. I think,' he said ironically, 'that we need a rest more than a restful girl. Isn't that it?'

Muller's left eye was still twitching. 'That's about it.'

The marshal shook his huge head. 'I like to help the workers – you came here with a Special Industrial Permit didn't you? – but you can't get a rest cure on a Blue holiday. You've got to be a White man at least.'

'It's difficult,' agreed Muller. 'But nothing else was available. I thought somehow I'd be a Red.'

The marshal shook his head dubiously, and Muller produced Mr Sims' wallet. 'They *don't* know,' he told himself, 'the office woman *hasn't* given the game away, but nonsense of that sort wouldn't come off with the marshal.'

'If I could have one restful day to start with,' he suggested, hesitating, then handing over most of Mr Sims's money.

'The fee is five but let's say twenty.' The marshal pocketed the money. 'Right. One restful day to start with. I'll try to make it two but I don't promise. The Red marshal's a bastard and I've heard a chief inspector's nosing around.'

'Chief inspector?' asked Muller as they walked down the drive.

'Office of Assessment. You know what *that* means. My nose is clean of course. Nothing to worry about except the death penalty.' The marshal sniffed judicially (his nose, if clean, was bulbously fiery) and adjusted his step to Muller's laboured walk. 'And strictly speaking, of course, you're a case for the medics. How you've escaped them I don't know. You must have influence.'

'Just a bit,' panted Muller.

'Anyway we'll try a morning in the baths. The Azo treatment in the Class I baths takes some beating.'

A red-haired nude with brown pubic hairs smiled provocatively from the door of a blood-coloured chalet, and the marshal sniffed.

'Cow. One of the Red marshal's sluts.'

'They don't seem to feel the chill,' said Muller.

'They'll feel it when the inspector gets into them. And *that* won't take long I assure you.'

Muller approached the Regenerative Baths with considerable trepidation. Such establishments were run usually by athletes for athletes, or at least, for men massively masculine; what the attendants would think when they saw his emaciated body he hesitated to consider. A bath on the other hand would do him good and would pass the time splendidly, so the risk was worth while.

But there was no need to worry. The attendants received him suavely and respectfully in the manner of the most superior hairdressers, and the Director of Treatment cluck-clucked sympathetically. 'You do look just a little run-down, sir. But leave it to us and don't worry. We'll have you on your feet in no time with our rectro-glandular treatment, but we'll start you off gently on Azo 3. It will remove the stress and strain and that's our first objective. *Then* we can make a start on the seminal ravages and so on.'

It was quite delicious. A needle slid into Muller's apprehensive arm and they gave him a tumbler of milky-looking stuff that made him tingle. He lay back in the tank – about eight feet by four – of golden water with foreboding, and for a time he was tossed about more violently than a cork in a mill race. He gasped and panted and tried to claw at the tank. Then, quite suddenly, the hurricane ceased, and he lay back, floating on the water, with a feeling of intense peace. He was like a man without a care in the world, a man who had enjoyed a pleasant evening, and was lying on the most luxurious bed imaginable.

'The storerooms,' Muller thought hazily, 'the storerooms must be loaded with food: enough to last me for months.' If this was a little game of Jallen's (and how could it be: for what purpose?) re-arrest was inevitable, and just as inevitable if he was genuinely a fugitive. Either way it could only be a question of hours, or days.

'It should be easy enough to steal a load of food, and that,' Muller told himself, as he floated silkily, 'left only one problem: where to make for?' A ruined town would be best, but to find one in the dark would be difficult, and there was unlikely to be water. In the hills and valleys (or what was left of them: bizarre pinnacles and crevices) water was a probability, and even wood, for making fires. 'Water,' Muller told himself, as he lazed luxuriously, 'water and food and fire.' It was a problem as old as history. But history, in 1999, had a habit of repeating itself. When a town was destroyed the survivors pulled out: and looked for fire, food and water.

*

He waited until the last light went out, then he circled the camp slowly, keeping just inside the boundary fence. It was deliciously cool now after a warm day, and the breeze from the sea mixed piquantly with the vapours of the camp. Muller himself felt cool and considerably rested, and although his legs were still numbed and tension was creeping up his shoulders and neck the day had done him good. After a light lunch – served in the Baths dining room – he had returned to the chalet and slept like a log until 9 p.m.

The gate adjoining the Hall of Joy was locked. It wasn't a high gate, but Muller couldn't scale it. It took quite a time to find something (an empty plastic drum) that helped him negotiate it: he landed heavily on the other side, and lay still for a moment, breathing heavily. 'Gates,' he muttered to himself. 'Why the gates and why the fence?' The campers could (up to a point, and within reason and with permission) leave the camp, but who without authorization might try to enter it? 'Who indeed?' muttered Muller, walking slowly and carefully, and hugging the wall of the hall. At last he reached the kitchen door and inserted the key: there was no response.

He stood thinking for a moment. The office was about eighty yards away, just out of sight, with staff bungalows beyond. Someone was bound to be in the office, but he (or she) was probably asleep, or sectically enthralled, and there was no sign of a nightwatchman. 'Don't be overcautious,' Muller told himself. He walked to his (or was it 'the') car and reversed it until the bonnet was directly below the window he had broken the previous morning. Soon he was in the storeroom, and the back of the car was loaded with food, cheeses and milk, egg, and meat concentrates mainly. Panting and sweating, he surveyed his work, then returned to the storeroom and filled most of the front of the car with packages of meat pies. As an afterthought he entered the building for the last time, and, with the help of the torch he had bought after leaving the Baths, searched the kitchens for cutlery and cooking utensils. It took some time to find a saucepan of manageable size. He found one at last, in a chef's cupboard. There were towels, too, and tablecloths. He dropped into the driver's seat of the car and wiped his forehead with one of the towels. As his breathing eased he touched the steering wheel tentatively: hardly had he done so than he saw the lights of cars approaching quickly up the coast road. For a few seconds Muller sat petrified; then he heard the shriek of a Blip, a shriek that became a snarling whine as the plane descended.

It landed about thirty yards in front of the car. Muller, crouching low, heard two men jump out, and the cars drive up. The speed of it was amazing. Doors slammed, there was a clipped order, and the sound of men marching away. There was silence for a few seconds, a hum of voices, and heavy feet again, barely audible, as the men marched down the drive. Muller, his heart beating wildly, sat up. In three or four minutes the hunt would be on. Jallen was in charge of the party; there was no mistaking that voice. He had called at the office to confirm or collect the chalet numbers, and a guide, and would soon be at the chalet. 'This is it,' Muller told himself. It wouldn't be long now. Shakily he gripped the steering wheel and pressed the starter button.

Chapter 9

The two apartment blocks marked the town centre. The coast road was on the right: the left fork was linked to the magnostrat. For less than a second Muller hesitated, then he turned left and jabbed the power button, streaking back towards Wapsaw. His jaw tight, he held the wheel grimly, the tyres screaming as the road dipped and curled. 'This,' Muller told himself, 'is the way in which I'll die. Nothing more certain.' But, after ten miles or so, the road joined the magnostrat, and, at 140 m.p.h. there was little sensation of speed. Forty miles from R3 Muller stopped. He felt as though he had drunk a lot of whisky and was roasting in front of a furnace. Every fibre of him was burning.

His legs were unsteady when he got out of the car. Shakily he leant against it and looked up at the sky. There was nothing about, absolutely nothing. He got back into the car, switched on the headlamps, and bumped slowly on to the concreted fields. They looked fairly flat and even. Muller turned off the lights and headed north, keeping his foot as lightly as possible on the power button, and straining his eyes for obstacles.

He tried to ask himself what Jallen would do. The point was that Jallen had gone to the camp looking for a man in a chalet, not a man in a car. When they found the chalet empty would they think at once of the car? They might, but they were more likely to search the camp, and to find out when he was seen last. At dawn certainly a full search would be on, and scores of Blips would look for him from the skies. It was a fine night and there would be little mist at dawn. The big black car would stand out as though the ground – eerily grey now in the moonlight – were covered with snow.

His initial idea had been to drive south and to conceal the car near the sea. His knowledge, geographical and topographical, of modern England was rather scant, as was almost everyone else's, but it had been a favourite topic of a friend of poor McAllister, and Muller remembered him saying that the area north of R3 was a vast marsh, and that the Welsh hills had been grotesquely convulsed by megaton bombing. It had seemed simple, and the time factor was vital. He couldn't go north, so he had to go south, and the hills were conveniently near to R3. The car had to be hidden, and hidden quickly: if it was found they would know he wasn't far away. There was no point at all in retaining the car, but it had to be hidden, and it might well be a vital asset in the future. Muller had expected no trouble in hiding the car. 'It had to be hidden so it couldn't be seen from the air, and there must,' he had thought, 'be an overhanging shelf of rock, or a cave or something of the sort,' into which he could easily drive it. He would store the food in the cave, and sleep in the car, and there would, of course, be water near by, and pools, perhaps, full of uncontaminated fish. It had seemed simple; childishly simple.

*

In thirty minutes he had covered about three miles. He had the door open now and was driving across what once had been ploughed fields or pasture land on the slopes of foothills. The heavy and immensely powerful car wallowed like a frigate, waddling over corrugations and heaving across the depressions of ancient ditches. Twice Muller hit something, the foundations of old walls probably; his heart thudded monotonously as the car dipped and heaved; the packages of food thumped against each other and the pans jangled somewhere on the floor. At length Muller stopped. 'This,' he told himself, 'is no good.'

When he had left the magnostrat his idea had been to skirt the tidal swamp in a great arc and to hide on the north-west coast. Jallen, he had thought, would be less likely to look for him higher up the coast: there was no direct road link between North Wales and the English north-west coast because of the great swamp. It was the best idea, obviously, but in two or three hours it would be dawn.

Muller climbed out of the car and looked about him. The ground sloped rather sharply to the right, and, in the distance – half a mile away, perhaps – was a line of hills, darkly impressive humps by night, but the sort of hills (Muller thought) that sloped more or less gently up and down, with little scope for cover. Muller hesitated. *If* there was a good chance of cover the best plan would be to journey in easy stages, hiding the car by day and covering twenty or thirty miles each night until he reached his objective. It was not only a good plan, it was tempting; but Muller looked around him, and looked at the car, which now seemed enormous. Supposing he had to hide the car, and hide it now, at this moment? He shivered, and scrambled back into the driver's seat.

'What can I *do*?' he asked himself, 'what can I do? I've got to do the opposite of what they might expect me to do, and do it quickly.' There wasn't time now to make for the ravaged coast south of R3, and there wasn't time to seek refuge in these hills. 'Hills,' Muller told himself reluctantly, 'are out; so is the coast.' There were on the other hand many bombed-out towns near Wapsaw, the countryside around Wapsaw was drearily flat, and it was, surely, the last direction in which they would look for him.

He trod on the starter and swung the car round. It kicked viciously, and Muller hit the roof. Wedging himself against it (the car was long and wide but very low-slung) he held the steering wheel with one hand, and jabbed the power button sharply and intermittently. He couldn't see a thing, and the car bounced and slewed like a maddened grasshopper. In five minutes it was back on the road: Muller flopped into the driver's seat, and dabbed his head, which was bleeding. 'I'm not realistic but, by God, you've made me a driver,' he muttered.

Pressing the button firmly he held his breath as the car screamed along at the best part of 200 m.p.h. He was holding the wheel much too rigidly, but the almost-straight road was a milky wraith that seemed to hold and control him as though he were glued to it, or to the silvery flash of the magnetic strip that snaked (it seemed) past his right ear. His head roared with the engine and his voice seemed to roar above everything. 'I'll do it in twenty minutes,' he shouted to himself, 'twenty minutes or fifteen minutes or maybe even ten minutes, if a Blip doesn't spot me, and I'll see Wapsaw again, or the lights of Wapsaw, the street lights and the glare above Arm T. Arm T! Arm T!' His tension increased, his head was held so stiffly, and so close to the wheel, that he was less than two miles from Wapsaw before he saw the glow. Removing his foot from the power button he let the car hurtle on for a few hundred yards before he applied the brakes. The tyres shrieked and he sat shaking with emotion.

For a few minutes he stared at Wapsaw, then he touched the power button and swung the car to the left. Steering was difficult: the car bobbed and swayed, and his hands were still trembling slightly. 'Better stop,' he told himself; his mouth was horribly dry again and his heart seemed to have increased enormously in size, and to have moved to the middle of his chest. Holding his chest he tried to think. There were many ruined towns thirty miles or so north of Wapsaw, and the going shouldn't be too difficult. For the first fifteen or twenty miles the countryside was dead flat, then there was a range of hills, but they weren't formidable. Old obstacles such as ditches and walls should now be little more than bumps or shallow depressions, and it should be easy enough to hide the car in the shell of an old building. But it had to be done in the dark and only an hour or so of darkness remained. The time factor was vital, and it was against him. 'I have sixty or ninety minutes,' Muller told himself, 'sixty or ninety minutes in which to cover twenty or thirty miles and to find the ruins of an old town.' The former would be easy; the latter difficult.

Muller plucked his lower lip. How did one find the ruins of a bombed town – in the dark, and from the driver's seat of a low-built car? There was only one answer: by road. The car now was (Muller hoped) facing north, and the ruins of the old Potteries towns lay about thirty miles due north. Muller was sure of this fact because the Potteries were thirty miles north of Wapsaw, and the car, as it now stood, was at right angles to Wapsaw, and parallel with the magnostrat to the north, which ran through the centre of Wapsaw. The Potteries were now defunct, and not, therefore, connected to the northern magnostrat, but the ruins couldn't be more than a few miles from the new road. It was tempting. Wapsaw must be avoided, but it would be easy to cut across country and to emerge on the magnostrat four or five miles north of Wapsaw.

Muller hesitated. It was inviting; a twenty-five-mile drive up the northern magnostrat and a quick descent into the valley of the Potteries. (If the Potteries were, or had been, in a valley: he couldn't remember.) It was tempting, but, if he drove up the magnostrat, he would still have to *search* for the Potteries, and dawn was all too near. With dawn scores of Blips would scan the coast and the main roads, but it seemed to Muller highly unlikely that they would hover over the ruins of old towns such as the Potteries. The search initially would be concentrated near R3, and the first hour or so of daylight might not, therefore, prove fatal, Muller told himself, if he were near the ruins and not near the magnostrats.

He drove slowly at first, holding the wheel lightly as the car bobbed and swayed. Often the wheel spun from his hands and often it righted itself on its own accord. There seemed little need, in fact, to hold it. After driving slowly for five minutes or so without incident Muller took a risk and snapped on the lights. They showed a grey desert of almost infinite drabness and Muller shuddered.

Clicking off the lights he increased his speed and the car gouged like a great beetle over the petrified wastes. The cartons of food danced about and Muller cursed himself for not arranging them more securely. He was pondering the advisability of stopping and re-arranging them when a sizeable carton smacked into his head. Cursing, Muller stopped and climbed out of the car. As he did so he noticed something about the sky that horrified him. He stared, unable to believe his eyes. But there could be no mistaking the strange light in the sky. It was dawn, the first unearthly pallor of dawn.

Muller's chest muscles tightened and his heart tremored with the old familiar palpitation. He had banked on another hour or so of darkness, thinking for some obscure reason that dawn was around 5 a.m. It was unbelievable: he of all people should know the time of dawn. Cursing himself he shakily jumped back into the car and jabbed the button. The great car seemed to float over the uneven ground, and Muller reassured himself with the thought that speed suited the damn thing, that dawn was only just breaking, and he hadn't far to go. There was no question about it: driven slowly the car wallowed like an old coaster, but at speed it seemed literally to fly over the concreted fields, soaring from bump to bump like a balloon. 'I'll do it easily,' Muller told himself. Staring intently ahead he increased pressure on the power button, and the car sang. But not for long. It tilted sharply to the left and there was a shriek of metal as the off-side wheel sank. For a second the car seemed to take root, then it ejected itself violently and slewed round, skidding sideways – in the direction of Wapsaw – for fully a hundred yards.

With a shaking hand Muller freed himself from the cartons – he was covered with meat powder – and climbed out of the car. He leant against it for a few seconds, then he walked slowly around it. The thing wasn't scratched; but the front off-side tyre had burst and the wheel hung limply.

'That's that,' thought Muller. He was still shaking and he sat down heavily. There was no question of fitting a spare wheel. The car was listing badly and the thing to which the wheel was attached was bent. Muller shuddered. He had – at 80 m.p.h. – seemed to be soaring silkily, but as he looked around him now, he saw a pocked and hillocked landscape that had probably been some form of rough moorland. In the distance he could see a small rocky outcrop, two or three concrete-encrusted boulders forming a triangular-shaped cluster.

After a few minutes Muller walked across to where the car had foundered. The concrete was gouged with cart-track-type runnels and there was a long rut, narrow but deep. Slowly and thoughtfully Muller walked back to the car. He was stilted with tension and his head throbbed sickeningly but he felt quite calm.

He stared at the food cartons. The powders were highly concentrated; a smallish bundle should keep him going for weeks. Slowly, like a man in a trance, Muller made up a bundle of food. He tore a table cloth in half, filling one half with meat powder and the other with milk powder. He dropped the parcels into another table cloth, adding (as an afterthought) the small saucepan. It wasn't a large bundle and it wasn't heavy, fifteen pounds or so, but he lifted it with difficulty. The dead, acutely exhausted feeling was spreading through him again.

He shouldered the bundle and set off. It was a last chance and a small one. Hiding by day and walking by night he could still reach the coast. But it wouldn't be easy to find places of concealment, and the Blips would be over at any minute. Muller stopped and turned, staring back at the outcrop. It was small, conspicuous, and so near to the car – not much more than two hundred yards away – that they were unlikely to think of him hiding there.

The ground rose quite steeply. Muller struggled up to the outcrop, and found a gap between the boulders, a gap about five feet long, but narrow. He squeezed into it with difficulty, dragging the bundle with him. He had to untie it and reshape it – sausage fashion – before he could ram it into the gap. He lay finally with his chin resting on it and part of it pillowing his chest. Breathing heavily, his heart pounding, Muller stared down at the car. He stared fixedly, gulping air now and then. For two hours at least he stared and nothing had happened. He closed his eyes and slept.

Chapter 10

When he awoke the sun was high and two Blips were standing near the car. The crews were watching the sky. Muller blinked and tried to stretch his neck, which was aching badly. As he did so two more Blips landed, and Jallen climbed out of one of them. He walked quickly – very quickly – to the car and inspected it. His examination was brief. He glanced into the car, walked around it, and marched away. As he did so the crew of the second plane descended on the car.

Jallen's cap was low and his face grim. In widening circles he walked around the car, staring at the ground, then he climbed a hillock and gazed about him. Muller buried his face into the bundle and tried to squeeze farther into the gap. They would have to be very near – two or three yards – to the outcrop to spot him, but it seemed impossible to believe that they wouldn't do so. Muller had gambled on the belief that the police wouldn't even inspect the outcrop because it was so near to the car and so obvious, and because they (presumably) thought him a clever man. After a few minutes there was a crunch of footsteps, and Muller saw the fault in his reasoning. A clever man, surely, would (unless he was injured) attempt to hide in a totally unexpected place. His heart beating wildly, Muller waited, but the footsteps stopped four yards or so from the outcrop. For two or three minutes there was silence, then the sound of more men approaching.

'Well?' snapped a voice – unmistakably Jallen's. It had never sounded more harsh and frightening.

'Well, sir,' someone answered rather tiredly, 'I don't think he was injured.'

'Of course he wasn't injured,' snarled Jallen. 'Why tell me the obvious?'

'Yes sir,' the detective said hastily. 'Well sir, Jarle here is an expert. He thinks the car was travelling north and –'

'North?' snapped Jallen.

'Yes sir. He may even have been circuiting the town, or heading for it. In my opinion –'

'Your opinion's idiotic,' snapped Jallen. 'Would anyone circuit a town at 90 m.p.h.?'

'It's possible sir. In any event he has a good start. Six to ten hours according to Jarle. The air-springing fluid has drained away but the fracture in the pipe is so small that Jarle thinks –'

Jallen stopped the detective with a noise like an angry tiger. There was the sound of feet crunching up and down, then silence for a few seconds as (presumably) Jallen stood and pondered. Muller, his heart bumping sickeningly, held his breath, and the detective coughed and said: 'Six to ten hours. That means he's anything from twenty to thirty miles away unless –'

'Five miles, you idiot.' Jallen spoke with a cold venom. 'Four probably and six or seven at most. After that he'd collapse. That means he's hiding somewhere. Find him. And quickly.'

Jallen marched away. There was silence for a few seconds, then someone (Jarle presumably) said: 'Well, he released him, didn't he, sir?'

There was an expressive grunt, and a weary – as the detectives walked away – 'It's the age of miracles, my lad. Come on.'

*

The Blips took off and Muller waited. His ribs and head ached and his legs felt dead. He had no feeling of hunger, but his throat was dry and his lips were sore. He tried to lick his lips but his tongue was unresponsive: it felt numbed and swollen. 'Must try to reach water,' Muller told himself. If it rained he could collect water in the saucepan, but there was no promise of rain.

The boulders met at the top, and he couldn't be seen from above, but the Blips searched feverishly. Dozens of them – as Muller stared into the distance above the roof of the car – crossed and re-crossed the sky, their engines shrieking as they soared and hovered. An immense roar announced the arrival of the armoured cars, fully a hundred of them in line abreast. Weird coronet-shaped things with tracks on telescopic stilts, they advanced slowly as they wheeled and counter-wheeled, opening and contracting their line, so that they were sometimes within inches of each other, and sometimes thirty feet apart. As they passed each side of the rock, their telictip sights glaring, Muller closed his eyes and tried to contract his ears.

By mid-afternoon the search had moved north; apart from an occasional Blip streaking back towards Wapsaw, all was quiet. Slowly and painfully Muller tried to turn about, so that he was lying on his back. He found it impossible. His legs were dead and his arms were badly cramped. The gap at the base of the boulders was little more than twelve inches wide and it narrowed sharply and triangularly. There was only one thing for it, but the first essential was to be able to move at all.

The concrete had trickled unevenly down into the gap, leaving many little lumps and hollows. Muller clenched and unclenched his fists in an effort to restore circulation, at the same time trying to wedge his feet firmly in the hope that his whole body might respond to his effort of will. After a few minutes the blood began to throb, and he started to inch out of the gap, pushing the bundle before him. His legs still felt dead, but he could move his feet quite freely, and his arms throbbed fiercely but they were fully responsive. For ten or eleven hours knobbly lumps of concrete had pressed into his body, and the pain was excruciating as the pressure was withdrawn. Breathing raucously, Muller clawed his way out of the gap: if a Blip spotted him it would be too bad, but it was a risk that had to be taken.

As quickly as he could – the sunlight was blinding –

Muller unfastened the bundle and tossed the saucepan and the meat powder into the gap. Then he followed, holding the parcel containing the egg powder in one hand and wriggling it under his head. Squirming about in an effort to avoid the lumps of concrete, he lay flat on his back with his eyes closed and his mouth open, breathing quickly and heavily. For quite some time he didn't move, then he opened his eyes and sprang up in terror, crashing his head on a boulder. When he had lain on his stomach he had been able to stare out into the open, but he was in almost total darkness now, in a living tomb.

He tried to drop back, and to resume his former position, but his shoulders jammed. Writhing frenziedly he freed himself. Hunching his shoulders he turned on his side, his chest heaving, his head streaked with sweat and blood. 'God,' he gasped. 'Oh, God.' The hysteria mounted and he started to claw out into the open, but he had moved no more than a few inches when a group of Blips skimmed the rock, streaking towards Wapsaw. The scream of their engines recoiled from the back of the gap with explosive force, and Muller was transfixed. Then – as the shriek mounted, and seemed to continue, within his head – he was convulsed almost epileptically, his eyes wild, his mouth gaping.

Worming into the open he lay with his head and shoulders revealed, his fists clenched as shock after shock seemed to pass through him. After a few minutes another formation of Blips flew over, travelling east to west. They didn't spot Muller, but the shriek of their engines, instead of worsening his dementia, in some way seemed to help him. His body gave a last tremor, and, for a time, he lay quite still. The main battle now seemed to be a struggle for air, the oxygen his over-taxed heart and lungs needed, but couldn't take in.

For twenty or thirty minutes he lay in the shadow of the rock. Blips – singly and in formation – flew this way and that, but they were travelling fast and high, with no interest in the area near the car. Muller took a long deep breath and propped himself up. Blinking wearily, he stared at the car. 'It's time I faced the inevitable,' he told himself; 'that I should be dead, that I must kill myself, or that I must die.' Staring at the car Muller tried to think about it, but his mind was hazy. It seemed years, not weeks, since he was free, and weeks, not days, since he was released. The hardest facts of all seemed the most difficult to accept, or believe, and he could not accept, even now, that McAllister was dead. But McAllister *was* dead, and McAllister would have been the first to emphasize that there was no point at all in going on, that further suffering was useless.

Slowly Muller wriggled back into the gap. He lay near the opening, resting on his right shoulder. 'They must capture me,' he told himself. 'Capture me and kill me. Nothing is pointless. I've beaten them so far, the dreamer, the visionary, the impractical man.' Groping with his left hand, he found the parcel of meat powder, and put a little of it in his mouth. It was dry, dry as dust, and Muller could produce little saliva. It needed an effort to chew carefully, but Muller chewed very slowly and very carefully until the dust became soggy, and the acrid mess took on a distinct meaty taste. As the food reached his stomach his jaws worked faster and he reached for more meat powder. This time he overdid it. Swallowing too hastily, he sat up sharply as some of the dust reached his lungs and the back of his nose. Coughing and sneezing violently he sat near the opening of the gap with the tears pouring down his cheeks.

At last – with a laugh – he wriggled lower down the gap, and made himself as comfortable as possible. He felt considerably better. After a few minutes his left hand touched something, and Muller frowned. 'It can't be,' he thought, feeling slowly and carefully, and his wonderment grew. There was something about the size of a saucer, something that felt deliciously soft and spongy. Muller explored with his fingers, touching and pressing, then he tore up a small lump. He held it delicately, squeezing it very gently, then he touched it to his forehead, and pressed it to his lips. There was no doubt about it. It wasn't chemical or some form of explosive, it was soil, virgin soil, a lump of mossy soil round which the concrete had trickled.

Muller was moved. His eyes moist, he sat up, holding the lump of soil carefully. He tried to think, but he couldn't think, and his memories were blurred. The seasons meant nothing now, but it was summer, a fine day in summer. On days like this his parents, when they were old, had sat out in the garden. Muller lay down again, pressing the mossy side of the soil to his lips. 'Once we had a garden,' he muttered. 'Once we had a garden.' When the next wave of Blips screamed over he was asleep.

*

He slept until about 9 p.m., then he rested quite peacefully until it was dark. The lumps of concrete prodding into his back and side were inconveniences that he scarcely felt. Everything was strangely muted. His body, though sick and weary, seemed remotely intangible, and his mind, though rational, seemed oddly distant. As night fell the Blips, singly and in groups, flew this way and that, their swirling arcs splashing great pools of light, but Muller felt in no way disturbed.

It was near midnight when he emerged from the gap, moving slowly and stiffly. When he stood upright the blood pounded in his head, and went on pounding for two or three minutes. Muller waited, then walked towards the car. Nothing was about, but the sky was savagely illumined to the east, and a distant rumble spoke of the activity of armoured cars. 'There's one place they won't look, not even with their telictip sights,' Muller said to himself, 'and that's the car.' The luxury of it after twenty hours in the gap was almost intoxicating, and he sat motionless for a few minutes, easing his aching limbs.

The food was still in the car, just as he had expected it to be, and Muller – as he rummaged for the meat pies – thought about it. The car, although repairable, was useless in its present condition and Muller could understand the police (at the moment at least) not bothering about it. It would for that matter be entirely typical of the times if no effort were made to reclaim it, if they left it to rot for ever. What was a car? What for that matter was a town? But the food was different. Hadn't it occurred to the police that he might hide near the car, and return to it for food? Apparently not. He was associated with the car, and they would assume that he would try to put as much distance as possible between him and the car. It was characteristically unimaginative, but was Jallen himself unimaginative? Muller wondered, and tried one of the pies. It was hard and unwholesome, and there was an unmistakable smell of rottenness. The chemically composed food, once it was processed, deteriorated quickly. Muller tried several of the pies and at last found one that was fairly soft and palatable. He ate a little of the centre, chewing very slowly and carefully. His tongue felt blubbery and hot sand might have stung his throat. He needed water.

For a long time he sat thinking. When he had left the gap he had intended to make up another bundle of food and set off at once towards the Welsh coast. He needed exercise and he had been looking forward to the walk. But he wouldn't – in his condition – be able to walk far, ten miles or so at most, and he would have to find another hiding place before dawn. There was no certainty of finding one, and exercise would increase his need for water. If he didn't find a hiding place, he would be spotted, and quickly. They were concentrating on the north, and the north-east and north-west, but the Blips were ranging wide: ten miles to a Blip was nothing.

An obvious solution was to stay where he was, hiding in the gap by day and resting in the car at night. There was plenty of food, and if it *did* rain the concreted ruts would be full of water. Muller didn't like the idea; he didn't *want* to stay where he was, but it was comfortable in the car, and for exercise he had only to walk around it. If it rained ten or twenty miles to the west it would rain here, and the gap seemed completely safe. In a few days the police might call off the search, thinking he was safely in hiding (in Wapsaw probably) or dead in a hole in the ground. For the second time in twenty-four hours Muller laughed.

He walked back to the gap and groped for the saucepan. He walked slowly and painfully and his breathing was laboured. It seemed mad to think of walking to the coast, but Muller wasn't despondent. His primary need was liquid. With water he would be better. With water he would be able to eat. There was comfort in the car, and warmth, if he could find the heater switch without turning on the lights. Would anyone who had known him believe that he could have endured the last few weeks? But many people had seen him and few people had known him; and they had seen (just as the police had seen) a *physically* unimpressive man. Muller stood the saucepan on a slight protuberance and returned to the car.

The engine responded at once and he found the heater switch without much difficulty. As the warmth soaked into him his body ached savagely – as though it had been kicked and pummelled – and his face felt strangely bloated. Muller's head nodded, but he didn't sleep. He felt like a man who had been on a riotous bender, but he warned himself not to sleep. It might be fatal; he might sleep well into daylight, and be spotted walking back to the rock.

For twenty or thirty minutes he told himself not to sleep. The next thing he knew it was daylight and the sun was shining wanly. Alarmed, he scrambled out of the car and made for the rocky outcrop. In his haste he forgot to turn off the heater.

Chapter 11

No sooner was he back in the gap than he regretted not deciding to set out for the coast. After the warmth of the car it was cold, bitterly cold, and lying on the concrete hurt badly. Shaking violently, Muller stared out at the rather dismal morning, and pressed a hand to his stomach. It was horribly, icily, nauseously empty, and his tongue felt like corrugated cardboard.

Not for five minutes at least did he notice that the concrete outside had a wet look, as though it had been raining. On hands and knees he scrambled out of the gap, and inspected the saucepan. Yes, there was a good inch of water in it. Thankful and excited, he lifted the saucepan as carefully as possible – his hand was shaking – and made for his hole. He deposited the saucepan to the side of the opening, and slid into it on his backside. But he couldn't reach the saucepan. After various contortions he turned over, and, lying on his belly, inched out towards the saucepan. Prodding himself on an elbow he reached for the saucepan, but his elbow was wobbling badly, and his free hand was unsteady. Cursing himself, Muller crawled out of the gap, and sat with his back to the rock. Lifting the saucepan with both hands he sipped two or three drops carefully; then he drained the saucepan and withdrew to his hole.

The effect was dramatic. The first drops of water seemed tasteless, but the full draught sank through him like jelly and caressed his system like wine. For two or three minutes Muller felt intoxicated, as though he had swigged a half-bottle of wine, then his stomach quivered and turned to ice. Lying on his back he shook uncontrollably. He couldn't have been colder if it had been the bitterest winter weather and he had been drinking iced water. His teeth chattering, he shook helplessly. His mind seemed as numbed as his body; and as helpless.

The weak sun vanished and it became overcast. There was no sign or sound of police activity, and the silence was absolute. After a time Muller began to feel it. Lying in his dark hole in the ground he began to tense. His trembling became less acute, then ceased, and his body tightened. The silence soaked into him with an obliteration of identity that mentally drugged him. As his physical tension increased his mind became more woolly, except for a small part of it that groped restively. It was as though a dark curtain had been drawn before him, separating him from the physical world and his own being. The fragment of consciousness that sought release probed delicately, persistently but vaguely seeking an outlet. A pinpoint of light seemed to roam an inert mass, floating hazily like a snowflake in an alley. For a time Muller seemed to be held in complete suspension, knowing nothing and feeling little. Then there was a sort of flash, physical and mental; with a shout he jumped up, again banging his head on the rock.

Trembling again, he dabbed his head, then rubbed his hands together. There was little feeling in them, so he wedged himself sideways, and rubbed them violently between his knees. He began to laugh, and stopped rubbing; for two or three minutes he laughed helplessly, tears running from his eyes and joining the trickle of blood down his forehead. He felt better for laughing – he was warmer and his stomach muscles were throbbing – and he remembered that some very old dog (as McAllister would have said) had given it as his opinion that deep anxiety was often the reason for laughter. 'I must be anxious,' Muller told himself; and he started laughing again.

It became even darker, and the rain fell, a trickle that became a steady downpour. Sitting on his haunches at the opening of the gap, Muller caught it in his saucepan, bathing his head with a piece of the tablecloth, and sipping now and then from the silvery saucepan. He felt like a great vintner sampling his wine. He laughed again; 'You're a fool,' he told himself, 'a crackpot, an idiot.' When the downpour slackened he tried to eat, champing steadily at the dusty meat powder. It was disgusting stuff; arching his tongue and licking his lips, he did his best to savour it, but most of it he spat out.

Gradually the morning brightened. The rain ceased and the sun glistened. Hugging himself tightly, Muller stared out at the concrete. With the sun near its height it looked dry and freshly washed; earlier it had steamed; during the downpour it had seemed inundated. 'The rain must drain away somehow,' Muller thought hazily, but he reminded himself that concrete was a minor question in an age of scientific perfection. It was undoubtedly porous. McAllister could have given him the answer, but it wouldn't have been a simple answer. McAllister some years earlier had threatened to write a novel with 'Smillie arose and put on his rupture appliance' as the opening sentence. McAllister had answered the hoots of derision (and looks of disdain and suspicion) with: 'We have all this progress, and miracles in surgery and science and what not, but men still rupture their guts, and operations by the best surgeons often fail to hold the rupture in place. After one operation and a second operation and maybe a third operation the poor old sods have to fall back on a distinctly old-fashioned rupture appliance, and if a man's ruptured guts don't sum things up tell me what does.'

Pressing his arms round his legs, his chin to his knees, Muller stared out over the concrete. He had – quite naturally – been obsessed with the physical aspects of escape, but it occurred to him that he might be alone for a long time, and he wondered how he would react mentally. He had spent much of his life alone and his previous isolation may have helped him to endure Arm T. He was not – or he had not been – a man of action, but he had (until the car crashed) coped well with the situation following his release. He had felt better for the two days of activity, and they had, in all probability, saved his life, but the old

Muller could have done little with the situation. He had been conditioned by weeks of torture. The logic of it seemed confusing and contradictory, and Muller smiled when he remembered the little box of capsules. They would have helped – whilst they lasted; but he hadn't even thought of them for days.

It felt warmer, distinctly warmer, and Muller's head nodded. He was sure now that he would make good his escape, and survive. It wouldn't be easy, but somehow he felt confident. There would be the problems of food and shelter, and the question (at some future time) of re-entering society, but he didn't feel despondent. Somehow he would endure. 'How lovely' – he thought – 'life must have been for the dear old shipwrecked mariners.' There they were on a tropical island with palm trees, bread, fruit, wild pigs and (very handily) a huge chest of tools to play with. Muller's head gave a last nod over the concrete. He hadn't for long thought of God, but he had been deeply religious in his youth: perhaps he would be helped spiritually. Not for many years had there been any public profession of faith; there had been no official opposition to religion after the nuclear war, but the churches hadn't been rebuilt, physically or spiritually. The survivors weren't interested.

'It's an interesting proposition,' thought Muller, as he drifted into sleep. At one time they had wanted to build Jerusalem in England's green and pleasant land, and a poet – now who was it? – whose name he couldn't remember had pictured Christ walking on the water – not of Gennesareth but Thames. But if Christ came again he would, almost certainly, have to walk on concrete and there could be no more splendid opportunity of transforming what was left of the world than to make the concrete green and pleasant again. Muller could testify to one irrefutable fact about concrete: it was hard.

*

He came to gradually, twitching convulsively as he alternated between varying levels of consciousness. He had one dream after another, some of them terrifying and obscure, and some of them associated with memories of the past. McAllister appeared often, and there could be no doubt of McAllister or the dubiety of his listeners. 'If you don't meet officialdom at its own level or in its own manner,' he was saying in one dream, 'fate won't be fickle or ironical: it'll be homicidal. Now take Jad Betty.' Someone made a noise, and McAllister retorted with: 'You're quite right. That's the reception he had. Not that he was that type of man – and he's been dead a long time. But some things persist of course. Jad – an undoubted genius – persisted, and you must bear in mind that he lived at a peculiar time. Two-thirds of the populace adored the monarchy and one-third of the aristocracy were renouncing their titles. But Jad produced his *God Help me! I'm a Rag-Picker* only to find that free libraries were springing up all over the place, and that the book-buying public had become the book-borrowing public. Jad protested – in his own manner of course – and what happened?' There was the inevitable silence and the inevitable: 'We don't know. You tell us.' 'I'll tell you,' said McAllister. 'They built more and more libraries with less and less book space and poor old Jad's works weren't included. He became a street-sweeper. Now one day – this was in Wapsaw of course – the Chief Librarian was sitting in his office when a chair came flying through the window. Now mark that,' McAllister exhorted. 'I don't have to tell you that chairs are kept *inside* buildings, so if a chair is to be thrown it will be thrown *out* of a window, and not into it. But this chair came crashing through the window, and I needn't remind you that experts still argue about that chair. The ownership is still doubtful and so is the origin, and there's been much speculation about the boy across the street. Some idiotic teenager who walked away laughing. Well of course everyone dashed outside and there was old Jad resting on his broom. Now –'

Muller's body gave a final jerk and he woke up. Startled

and confused, he fumbled feverishly, then – realizing where he was – he sank back on his haunches, staring muzzily at a patch of concrete and sky. He was sitting at an angle; his legs were twisted beneath him and his back (or part of it) rested against the boulder. After a time he uncurled himself and – slowly and painfully – pivoted around so that he was facing the opening of the gap. As the circulation returned to his legs they tingled and throbbed, and his head hammered sickeningly. Slowly it eased, and Muller – feeling like a man with a hangover – rubbed his eyes and stared at the car. The door was open and the list seemed more pronounced.

He sighed and reached for the saucepan. He put it to his lips but was ill-rewarded. With the pan still in his hand he remembered something about the car. The meat pies. He had sampled at least six of them and he hadn't attempted to hide the debris. Muller sat up sharply. If the police returned to the car they would see at once that someone had been sampling the pies. After thinking it over Muller relaxed. It was most unlikely that the police would look again at the car. Why should they? They had inspected it once, and they were looking for him, not the car. He relaxed, at the same time telling himself that he had been stupid. Staring at the car he wondered if it would be too risky to go out to it and tidy it up. As he stared he saw something approaching. It was a large black car.

Muller's heart stabbed violently but his mind moved like lightning. There was no mistaking the car – it was Jallen's – or the reason for the extreme slowness of its approach. Jallen was dissatisfied with the results of the search. He didn't believe that Muller could have got far. He had guessed that he was hiding near the wrecked car; and he was studying the line of its approach and the land around it. 'This time he'll get me,' thought Muller. There was nothing more certain. One look into the wrecked car and . . . Muller's face drained. He remembered now that he had not only given himself away with the meat pies; he had left the heater on.

Jallen's aide was driving and Jallen was staring intently. The aide swept in a slow circle around the wrecked car and pulled up alongside it. Jallen jumped out, looked about him, and peered into the car Muller had abandoned. He reacted like a man kicked violently. As the aide hurried to his side, Muller – on his hands and knees – scrambled out of the hole and crouched down on the other side of the outcrop. They hadn't seen him; the aide was gaping into the car and Jallen was behaving like a man demented. Muller licked his lips; it wouldn't be long now.

In three or four minutes he heard footsteps. They were approaching, and quickly. Another few seconds and there was a frightening roar.

'I knew it!' shrieked Jallen. 'I knew it, I knew it! Men and machines out for miles and he's been here all the time!'

Judging by the noise he appeared to be dancing up and down. 'It's incredible sir,' said the aide. 'He must have been here yesterday when –'

'Of course he was here!' cried Jallen. 'Of course he was here! And my best detectives helped him to stay here by blocking the hole with their backsides! But they'll pay for it!' he shrieked. 'They'll pay for it! I'll – I'll –'

He spluttered into incoherence, and the aide – after a cautious wait – said diffidently: 'It's an amazing thing, sir. Who would have thought that this man –'

'Man!' roared Jallen. 'He's craftier than Satan! Trickier than sin! He – he's . . .' and he became incoherent again. Muller could hear him stamping violently up and down. They weren't more than three yards from him and Muller knew it was the end. Crouching low, clawing the rock, he waited. They had only to step a few paces, they were sure to look behind the rock. But they didn't. And Jallen – when he spoke again – was more composed and the metallic chill was back in his voice. 'This has harmed me a lot. It will take some getting over. But it proves how right I was. What an enemy this man would be if he had backing!'

'Yes sir,' said the aide. 'You're quite right sir. But where do you think he is now?'

'Where!' snapped Jallen. 'In a better damned hole you idiot! This is no more than a crack. Look at it! So at dusk last night he'd hunt around and find a cave or something.'

'A cave?' said the aide. 'But if –'

'If!' roared Jallen. 'If!' He stamped up and down again. 'By God,' he said violently, 'what I could have done with a few men like Muller on my side!' There was a pause, then Jallen – more calmly – said: 'It must have been painful in here – even for a very thin man. So he'd look for a larger hole. He guessed that my prize idiots would expect him to be miles away, so he decided to stay close to the car.'

'Yes sir,' said the aide. 'I see, sir. He certainly seems to have spent the night in the car.'

'Seems!' snarled Jallen, almost demented again. 'Seems! There's food in it. Warmth! Comfort! Provided by – by –'

'Yes sir,' the aide said quickly. 'It's extraordinary. But he can't be far away.'

'Neither is the Congress,' snapped Jallen. 'It will have to be put off. I don't think Muller has accomplices but we can't take chances. Or' – his voice rose with hatred and disgust – 'perhaps I should say we can't afford to take *more* chances.' There was a brief silence and Muller could hear him striding towards him. As Jallen and his aide (walking anti-clockwise) moved to the rear of the rock Muller edged round to the front.

'Look!' said Jallen. 'See how the land over there falls away! That's it! A sort of valley. You can bet there's a cave or airshaft of an old mine or something of that sort. Come on! And this time,' he said malevolently as he walked away, 'this time I'll attend to Muller personally. We seem to have failed to have broken his mind so I'll take his body and. . . .'

Muller stood up. For three or four minutes he didn't

move. He was greatly tempted to crawl back into the hole, but the chances were that many officials would now visit it. Even if Jallen suppressed all news of it he would (probably literally) rub the noses of some of his detectives against the sides of the gap.

There was only one thing left. In the bright sunlight Jallen's car gleamed forebodingly. It looked immense and monstrous. Muller walked towards it.

*

He drove carefully. The dashboard bristled with equipment that enabled Jallen to see almost everything that went on. Whether *he* (against his wish) could be seen or heard was doubtful, but Muller stopped as soon as he saw a likely piece of rock, and smashed the row of apparatus. Breathing hard, he drove carefully towards the magnostrat. One of the shattered instruments emitted a low humming noise.

He thought hard. Jallen and his aide were unlikely to be carrying portable transmitting apparatus, and they would spend probably an hour or more searching the valley. They would be able to do nothing when they found the car missing; they would have to walk. It was possible of course – all too possible – that a roaming Blip would spot them, but Muller considered he had one to three hours in which to find refuge.

He was – once again – tempted to drive across country towards the Welsh hills and the sea, but there were the difficulties of the terrain and the risks of identification. The Blip pilots were all too familiar with Jallen's car, and they would – if they saw it – remain at a respectable distance. They would not, therefore, identify the driver. And they would think nothing of it if they saw Jallen's car streaking towards R3. But they might be curious – and more – if they saw Jallen's car fifty miles west of the magnostrat, or overturned on a Welsh hillside. Muller still preferred the idea of driving across country, but time was against him.

He smiled. For some unaccountable reason he felt quite calm and composed. His haggard, unshaven face was pale and set, but his eyes – for the first time for weeks – were soft and dreamy again, if somewhat ironic. Either course – across country or up the magnostrat – offered little hope, unless he could avoid R3 itself, and go quickly to ground, but he felt strangely assured. The Blips and the mechanical monsters were probably engaged in the north and east, and he (or Jallen's car) might not be seen at all. The ravaged coast south of R3 would hide him and he would overcome the problem of food. 'I'll eat grass,' Muller told himself, 'I'll eat grass if there's grass and seaweed if there's seaweed; I'll find a cave lined with sand and watch the sea and the stars. I may find something in nature and something in myself; a man had to be lost before he could find himself, and who could be more lost, personally and officially?'

He kept the gigantic car on as straight a line as he could, but he must have veered considerably to the south. The ground dipped sharply, and, once again, he saw the towers of the town. Muller stared for just a few seconds, then he turned sharply to the right, and screeched across the adhesive strips of the magnostrat. With a velvety sway the monster righted itself as the wheel spun viciously: Muller grabbed it and depressed his foot. With a tremendous *whoosh*! the car hurtled towards R3.

By-passing the town proved comparatively easy. Muller – driving with intense concentration – slackened speed when he was ten miles or more from the town. As soon as he saw the towers of the apartment blocks he braked, and swung the car to the left. He became tense and anxious again, and his neck burned fiercely, but the ground was reasonably negotiable, and the car crawled forward with ease. After penetrating about two miles to the south Muller turned westerly towards the sea. There were several hills now and unexpected little valleys. Time and again he had to stop and reverse, to probe to his left or his right, and in any direction that offered. It was another two hours at least before he bumped on to the old coastal road. The sea was spread out before him but he gave it no more than a glance. It was uninteresting; flat and grey, and he felt exhausted again.

Turning left away from R3 Muller drove quickly along the road. There was no sign of life. It hadn't been possible to watch the sky, and he had seen no other vehicle or any form of life. Away to his left the concrete ended, and, to his right now and then, he saw the beach and the sea, but he felt little response. Either way it was desolation, and his eyes were heavy. After a few miles the road wandered uncertainly through the stumps of a shattered town, and then (it had been disused for many years) petered out gradually. There were huge cracks and potholes, and clumps of weird-looking vegetation. Muller, staring anxiously and driving carefully, lost all traces of it after about two miles, and, for a time, crawled forward gingerly. Then he stopped.

There had been hills on his left and cliffs on his right. There were no hills now as such or cliffs as such. An immense subterranean force seemed to have thrown parts of the hills into the sea and some of the sea into the hills. As Muller – from the driver's seat – looked to his left he saw great gaps and water at different levels: to his right was not the open sea but blue water slapping around great rocks. The unreality of it was frightening. There were great voids to Muller's left and inlets of the sea snaking to oblivion. In the distance was a large lake, dreamily blue, and far below it a smaller lake of intense brilliance.

Muller left the car. He stood for a moment and walked slowly forward. Not fifty yards from the car was a gorge. There was a sheer drop of hundreds of feet with a channel of water far below. Muller stepped back sharply and wandered to his left. His feet dragged but not merely because of weariness. He could – very faintly – hear water slapping against rocks, but there was no other sound. The silence was primeval. Even the sound of the water increased his uneasiness. It was late afternoon and the tide

– he thought – should be out. If it was there would be no sound of water. The rocks may have cut off the sea partially or wholly. It was unlikely, and there would be little sound or movement from trapped water, but the answer lay probably in the sea bed. Muller walked more quickly to the edge of the chasm. It was immense; awesomely grotesque, but the effect, as he stared before him, was of nothingness. He felt infinitely exposed and alone.

He turned away and walked back to the car. It was oddly reassuring. He was tempted to get into it and drive back down the road. He couldn't possibly stay where he was. Nearer the ruined town there had been vegetation of a sort; there might be a hiding place there and some chance of keeping alive. Muller thought for a moment and shook his head. He had wasted time enough and he must get rid of the car. Sliding into the driver's seat he drove it carefully to the edge of the gorge; it took several minutes to find a suitably sized piece of rock, but the angle was difficult, and the door impeded Muller's aim. He managed at last to strike the accelerator button, and the car roared into the air. It seemed fully a minute before the smack of it hitting the water reached Muller; when he peered over the edge of the gorge the car was sinking fast.

Wearily he turned away. All he could do now was hide until morning. Finding a hiding place wouldn't be easy. Everything seemed glaringly exposed and glacial, but there must be a crevice or something down on the shore. He had taken no more than three tired steps when he heard a distant shrilling noise, a faint whistling that swelled quickly to the familiar shriek. Muller felt a faint pang and no more. Indeed he felt calm. For the first time for weeks he was without fear. From the rear he looked dishevelled and disjointed, an ageing, broken figure. But he stood calmly as they approached; his chin lifted slightly, and he smiled. The Blips dived, their rockets blazing.